# THE
# INFERIOR

---

## MARTA COFFER

*For Ellena —
Thanks for your help!*

*Marta Coffer*

Printed in the United States of America

First printing, 2013

ISBN: 1482527421
ISBN-13: 978-1482527421

www.CreateSpace.com

# Acknowledgments

With many thanks to my friends and family members who read and critiqued this book in its elemental stages and helped me bring out the best in it. And to Laura K. Cowan and my husband Jon – thank you for your constant encouragement, insight, honesty, and for sticking with me through all the mountains and valleys of this venture. Jon, thanks for encouraging me to "finish something."

[Since] the inferior always predominates numerically over the best, if both had the same possibility of preserving life and propagating, the inferior would multiply so much more rapidly that in the end the best would inevitably be driven into the background, unless a correction of this state of affairs were undertaken. Nature does just this by subjecting the weaker part to such severe living conditions that by them alone the number is limited, and by not permitting the remainder to increase promiscuously, but making a new and ruthless choice according to strength and health.

Adolf Hitler - <u>Mein Kampf</u>

# 1

Allison dragged in a breath of air that seared her lungs like fire. She wiped sweat from her forehead with the back of her hand and imagined her skin melting, her lungs collapsing....

"Get your skinny little butt moving!"

The roar amplified into a tidal wave of sound. Allison jumped and smashed her head against the metal ceiling of the duct. For a moment she held her spinning head still. Dark strands of hair fell from her ponytail to frame her face. She tucked them behind her ears and scrambled towards the dysfunctional fan at the end of the passage. Daylight jabbed at her eyes. She squinted through it and made out a thin string choking the fan blades. The protective grill on the other side was rusted firmly into place.

A utility knife emerged from one of the many pockets in Allison's grimy jumpsuit, and she snapped open the screwdriver. She held tightly to the grill as she twisted the stubborn, encrusted screws until they fell into her hand. She scraped off as much rust as she could, oiled them, and replaced them. Then she slashed through the offending string and watched the blades begin to rotate. Cool air washed over her face.

"Done," she sighed.

Allison used her elbows to push herself backward through the ducts. As she lowered herself through the opening into the machine room, a rough hand clamped around her ankle and yanked. Thin, metal edges dragged against her palms, and she yelped. The ladder she'd been aiming for fell over with a clatter, and Allison landed hard on the concrete floor, dark eyes wide with fear. Fat Face towered over her, a mountain of a man bulging out of his plaid shirt and worn overalls. Hard blue eyes glittered angrily in his red, fleshy face. He hunkered down in front of her, and she edged backwards a bit, cringing.

"When I tell you to do something," he hissed, "you do it fast. Got it?"

"Yes, sir," Allison whispered. She braced herself against the floor and winced as hot pain seared her hands.

"Now get out. I don't want your filthy blood all over my floor."

When she didn't move, he seized her ponytail with one meaty hand and pulled her to her feet. She squeezed her eyes shut against the pain that ripped across her skull and forced herself not to struggle. Fat Face propelled her head forward, let go abruptly, and she stumbled away from him. She landed on her forearms and knees with bone-jarring force. Mercifully she was able to keep her bloody palms off the floor. She sucked in a breath as waves of nausea rolled in her stomach. Anxious faces peeked out from behind the mighty machines on either side of them.

"Get out! All o' you rats!"

A dozen jumpsuit-clad adolescents scurried towards two metal doors set in the cinder block wall. Fat Face stalked off to his office and slammed the door behind him. As soon as he was gone, a tiny girl with wild brown hair emerged from behind a giant engine and rushed to Allison's side.

"Let's go now," she said softly as she took her friend's elbow and helped her to her feet. Allison trembled with shock and found it difficult to move very quickly. Her small friend held her tightly and guided her through the doors. Blazing sunlight hit Allison with all the force of a punch.

"Let me sit for a minute, Yanna," she said shakily. Her knees gave way, and she plopped down on the concrete step.

She rested her hands palm up on her thighs and stared at the jagged wounds. Yanna sat down close to her, watching her anxiously.

"Was this your first time here?"

"Yeah. I heard about Fat Face, but...."

"But it's hard to believe," Yanna finished for her. "I know. You wouldn't believe some of the things he's done. It's a good thing you didn't fight him. He would've pounded you into a pulp."

The wild-haired girl rummaged through her pockets and found a relatively clean rag. She flipped open her pocketknife, slashed the cloth into two long strips. Allison clenched her teeth and drew a hissing breath as Yanna wound the strips around her hands.

"Thank you."

"Sure."

The rest of their work group was disappearing between the ancient warehouses lining the alley. One of the guards assigned to the group looked back and yelled something unintelligible. He drew a short, thick piece of wood from his belt as he came striding towards the girls.

"Time to go." Yanna sprang up. "Think you'll make it?"

"Uh-huh." Allison got to her feet clumsily and walked slowly down the alley with her hands away from her sides. Yanna trotted at her side.

"What'd you think you were doing?" the guard growled as they approached him.

"Sorry, sir," Yanna spoke quickly, keeping her eyes lowered. "She got hurt, and I was helping her."

"Huh," he grunted, slipped the weapon into his belt and frowned darkly at Yanna. "Well, now we're off schedule. Get going!"

"Yes, sir."

Yanna took Allison's arm, and they edged past him. They trudged along in silence, the two girls in front, the sullen guard close behind. They followed a wide cracked road that ran straight between giant metal-sided warehouses. A caravan of yellow delivery trucks rumbled toward them, and the threesome moved aside to walk with their shoulders brushing a rusty metal wall. The trucks churned the air into a choking cloud of dust and fumes. Allison and Yanna buried their noses in their sleeves while the guard hacked and cursed incoherently. Then there was only the rumor of engines idling and men barking commands at each other. A sharp bend in the road led them past the last warehouse and opened into the colorful district of Lind Street.

The air exploded with color and sound; cars sped by, music blared from busy shops, thick mobs of people talked, laughed, and shouted as they went on their various ways. The group jumped aside to avoid a mad cyclist and hurried for the relative safety of the pedestrian lane. Striped canopies spread from the storefronts over the lane and made the hot day a little more bearable. A collage of delicate scents escaped from one open door to tease the noses of fashionable women. Allison was suddenly conscious of the stink of her own sweat and squeezed her arms against her torso.

A frazzled mother pushed a stroller by them. Every few seconds she turned her head to plead with her distracted toddler to stay close. Two middle-aged men in well-cut suits held a barely polite conversation they passed on the other side. Allison bumped into Yanna as she made room for them.

"If you had investigated the company before recommending they invest in it," one man spat out, "you would have seen it was on the verge of collapse."

"It wouldn't have collapsed," the other returned, "if your bank manager client hadn't called in their loan."

The two men strode quickly beyond hearing.

Arms entwined about each other, a young couple sauntered along, pausing to kiss or peer dreamily into shop windows. Children darted, skipped, and weaved among the grown-ups. They laughed and called silly things to one another while the adults smiled benevolently on them. Young and old, they all went around Allison and Yanna as though the girls were signposts. Their eyes were always fixed on something else, so Allison watched them with open curiosity. They couldn't see her. They wouldn't see the scarlet drops she left to blacken on the sidewalk.

The two girls passed an enormous stucco movie theater bearing large posters of a classic documentary, children's musicals, and the second installment of a mystery series. A pair of ornate wood doors burst open to spew a group of teenagers onto the sidewalk, where they clustered in a laughing, gesturing knot. Allison and Yanna slowed, seeking a way around them but unable to step into the busy street. They glanced nervously at the traffic, then back at the vibrant group blocking their way.

"Keep moving!" The guard urged them on with a none-too-gentle nudge toward the curb.

"He was such a great speaker!" a girl's voice drifted to them. "I wish I could remember what he said."

"Thomas does," said another, elbowing a tough-looking boy with a shock of sandy hair. "He's got a great memory. Give us a bit from one of his speeches?"

Thomas' eyes blazed with excitement. "'... the Party will materialize into an eternal and indestructible pillar of the German people and Reich.'"

· The teens clapped and begged for more. Allison and Yanna inched closer, trying to skirt the group.

"'Today we must examine ourselves,'" Thomas' voice rang out, "'and remove from our midst the elements that have become bad. And therefore do not belong with us!'"

The laughter and applause died down as Allison stepped gingerly along the very edge of the sidewalk. She glanced up. Hard, suspicious stares met her timid gaze. They murmured under their breath, drew back from the little group. Yanna linked her arm with Allison's and walked faster.

"...inferiors."

"Bad element.... don't belong in any civilized society."

The venomous tone struck Allison almost physically, and she cringed.

The guard snickered behind them.

It was with an unusual sense of relief that they crossed the last intersection before coming to the orphanage. It was an ugly building, seven stories high, a solid stack of concrete. The windows were tinted a murky shade, partly for privacy. Above the great double doors were imbedded the words "New Munich Orphanage for Inferiors." Flanking the tarnished letters were brilliant crimson and white flags with black, broken X's blazing from their middles. Allison hunched her shoulders involuntarily as she passed beneath them. Yanna struggled to push open the heavy door for her, and the three went inside. Allison stopped just inside to let her eyes adjust to the dim lighting of the lobby.

It was like a cave, with yellow lamps spread an unorthodox distance apart and stone-colored wallpaper. A long line of kids waited to be checked in by a stocky woman with a permanent frown. Watching them from strategic points were security guards in brown uniforms with small buttons bearing the broken X fixed to their caps. Their own guard pushed past them, sweeping his hat off his sandy hair and muttering under his breath as he stumped away. His counterparts nodded to him or called out greetings. Allison dropped her eyes and joined the line of orphans.

A group of tall boys burst through the entrance, swaggering and leaving a trail of sawdust and dried mud. Allison glanced swiftly at them, averted her gaze again. The orphans called these boys "giants" for their height and strength, and avoided them whenever possible. A bored, aggressive, six-foot-tall kid was no one to tangle with. The noisy group shoved their way to the front of the line. Most of the orphans wisely backed up a few steps, but one Asian boy stood dreaming near the desk. A massive giant with a flat face sent him sprawling with a casual fist to the head. The others laughed and crowded around Steiner's desk.

"One at a time!" she barked at them.

They jostled themselves into a ragged line. Allison peered around Yanna at the fallen boy. He staggered to his feet and rubbed his head as he went past her to the tail end. One of the guards smirked at the injured child, turned his head and made a dry comment to another guard. They never interfered with fights between orphans unless it looked like one might be in serious danger of losing his life. Then they would wade in, swinging their thick wooden rods. At such gentle persuasion, even the largest boys would step away from their victims. Allison turned her head away from these thoughts and steeled herself for a long wait.

The orphans inched forward until Allison found herself in front of the imposing desk, wilting under the gaze of Mrs. Steiner. At Steiner's gruff command she leaned forward for the retinal scan that identified her as A160434, an inferior orphan. She shifted her feet nervously while Steiner pecked away at the computer.

"Uh.... Mrs. Steiner?" Allison whispered.

"What!"

Allison cringed and forced herself to continue.

"I hurt my hands."

"Speak up, girl!" Steiner barked.

"My hands. I hurt my hands today."

"Let me see."

Steiner straightened to her full height. Allison's heart beat painfully as the big woman leaned forward and grabbed her wrist. She yanked at the edge of the makeshift bandage and peered at the jagged tear. Releasing Allison abruptly, she sat down again.

"Go to the nurse before decontamination," Steiner said curtly.

"Yes, Mrs. Steiner," Allison managed. She tossed a quick glance back at Yanna as she hurried down the hall to the nurse's office. Her friend gave her a wan smile and waved a little. Allison scanned the labels on the doors she passed and found the nurse's office was the fifth on the left. She was trying to figure out how to knock when the door swung open to reveal a trim little woman with a cheery face. Her golden blonde hair looked too perfect to be real, and her uniform was a brilliant white.

"Oh! You're here already," the nurse said in piercing tones. "Come in and let me have a look at you. Watch the door. Steiner called to say you'd be coming. I haven't had a patient in such a long time. Nearly two days now! Up on the table, please. Now don't think I want anyone to get hurt, it just gets lonely and boring. How smart of you to wrap your injuries! Let's take a peek, shall we? I really do like fixing children up. They're always so .... oh, dear! Those hands look terrible! Wait just a minute while I...."

The nurse went off to an adjacent supply room, talking happily to herself, and left Allison sitting on a padded table amidst numerous machines and instruments. As Allison looked around the spotless room, her eyes caught on a small mirror. She stared at the skinny stranger with huge brown eyes. Her skin was several shades lighter than her eyes, but much darker than anyone she'd seen outside the orphanage. In fact, Allison looked nothing like them. Neither did Sam, Faye, Neill, Roman, or any of the other kids.

The nurse came back with a glow of triumph on her wide face and a slim silver tool in her hand. She set a metal tray over Allison's lap and instructed her to rest her hands on it. Allison's mind withdrew from the nurse's inane chatter and relived the stinging words of the teens from the movie theater.

*A bad element. Why?*

Allison flexed her fingertips as she searched her memories. Grumpy matrons, disdainful teachers, and stone-faced guards had taken every opportunity to grind her inferior status into her mind. But they had never explained why, never mentioned what horrible crime her kind of people had committed against them. Perhaps it was too horrible to name.

An icy sensation blunted the pain and hushed it to a dull

throb. Allison focused on smooth white bandages. They looked like electrical tape. She closed one hand and discovered it moved without stiffness.

"All better," sang the nurse as she stuffed an extra bandage in a drawer. "Decontamination won't hurt those in the least. They're the latest thing – waterproof, medicated, and flexible. Just leave them on for twenty-four hours, and they'll peel off easily. You be more careful around those nasty machines now. They really ought to let grown-ups handle that sort of work. Off you go!"

Allison hopped off the table and left without looking back. She flitted inconspicuously through the busy lobby and slipped into the stairwell. She counted the gloomy windows at each landing as she climbed slowly up to the fourth floor. Other orphans pushed roughly past her, but there was no need to hurry; there was still a long wait for the heavy, black sliding doors that led to the decontamination chamber. Four men and women in brown uniforms patrolled the antechamber. They watched those entering the elevator-sized room and watched the doorway on the right where a few orphans exited the dorms and watched the snaking line of impatient orphans. Allison picked at the edges of her bandages, eyes glued to the heels of the girl in front of her.

Shuffle, shuffle, stop. Shuffle, shuffle, stop.

"Next. Next! I don't have all day!" the decontamination director bellowed.

Allison scooted into the black chamber and pressed the green button next to the doors on the opposite wall. Gases hissed down from tiny brass nozzles in the ceiling, tugging dirt and germs from her hair and jumpsuit in their strange downward breeze. She shivered with loathing and counted until the hissing stopped abruptly and the great doors slid open.

A narrow hall of cold marble lay before her, its impersonal walls studded with doorways at regular intervals. A few drab little figures pattered through the various openings. Since one normal footstep reverberated like a gunshot, Allison walked as softly as she could to the last doorway on the right. It was a long way for one going slowly, and she always felt that unfriendly eyes watched her every move.

She breathed a small sigh of relief as she crossed the threshold into her dormitory. Six standard cots lined the walls on either side, each separated by two grooved pillars. At the end of the rectangular room a square window gave a grudging view of the city. Four of Allison's roommates perched on their cots with food in their laps. Allison received a few glances of welcome as she went to her cot in the far left corner. Yanna, still munching some unidentified substance, gathered up her bread and crossed the aisle to join her friend.

"What'd she say about your hands?" Yanna asked after swallowing a piece.

Allison curled her legs underneath her and tucked a stray tendril behind one ear.

"They'll be fine. Bandages come off tomorrow evening."

"Did it hurt?"

"Uh…. not really."

"Last time I was down there she almost cut off my foot." Yanna wrinkled her nose, then grew serious again. "George hasn't come in yet. His group was supposed to be back an hour ago."

Allison glanced at the empty bed between Sam and Faye. The blanket was still bunched and wrinkled from last night. Her heart sank when she saw Sam's face twisted with worry, how he ate methodically and without appetite. Every so often his eyes shot to the doorway, then back to nothingness.

On a hunch, Allison asked, "Are those extra boots still under his bed?"

Yanna leaned forward, craning her head 'til she was upside down. "No, they're gone." She sat up, her thin face flushed and uneasy in the late afternoon light. "What does that mean? Somebody stole them?"

"I've got a bad feeling," Allison whispered, with a glance at

Sam.

"It's probably another thief. We should keep all our personal stuff in our pockets. Someone will probably complain, and they'll spend all day searching us." Yanna sighed her exasperation.

"And George?"

"He'll turn up."

A raucous clang sounded from the hallway, and chaos took over as everyone snatched up their leftovers and ran for the door. Allison looked mournfully at her uneaten dinner, then got up to deposit it in the hallway trash can with the others. Back at her bed, she tugged her shoes off, fished tools out of various pockets, and shoved them all under the bed. She curled up on her side with the scratchy blanket tucked snugly under her chin. The lights went out suddenly. A sickly twilight filled the room, interrupted by a stream of light pouring through the door.

The sharp rap of boots echoed from the hall, pausing from time to time as Steiner checked each room. They grew louder and louder until Steiner's shadow blocked the flow of light. The boots went off again, stopped, and a sharp cry pierced the air. Allison winced, pulled her blanket over her ear. Mechanical whirring filtered through the material as machines in the floor above came to life. Thick, black slabs descended from the ceiling, gliding down the grooved pillars to create tiny cells around each bed. They cut the light like guillotines and met the floor with one grim thud.

Allison shut her eyes tightly as darkness pressed in around her.

*I wish you were in here with me, Yanna,* she told her friend silently as she curled up on her side.

Silence greeted her thought with cold indifference, and she faced alone the same dream that haunted her every night.

*The Inferior*

# 2

**M**emory Square was very quiet on Sunday morning. The sleek office buildings exuded tranquility rather than efficiency; their glass walls reflected each other instead of government officials bustling around. The middle of the square was dominated by a bronze statue of a man with a small mustache, one arm extended toward the east. Allison decided it must be his fervent stare that kept all the government employees going, but she didn't have time to think anything else. She and a specially selected group of electricians had a job to do. The computers in a government department were down, which meant solitary confinement for the orphans if everything wasn't in perfect working order by Monday.

The chosen few marched behind a representative of the department. He was an ex-military type, Allison decided, with his stiff back and granite face that encouraged absolute silence. Four guards from the orphanage brought up the rear, like drill sergeants keeping their troops in order. Allison cast covert glances at the other orphans and noted that they all wore the same anxious-frightened expression.

By the time they reached the fantastically tall building at the end of the square, Allison's hands were shaking. Its gleaming facade of windowed walls climbed dozens of stories, tapered, then climbed, tapered to a golden spire just visible as a spark of light. Two uniformed custodians held the heavy glass doors open while their guide explained the problem in clipped sentences.

Metal detectors hovered protectively over the entry, which gave way to a spacious marble lobby dotted with fat, curving pillars. The hall was a long affair of spotless tiles, darkly-stained doors, and security cameras perched in odd positions. They rounded a corner, and the hall opened into a factory-sized room filled with row after row of desks, all of which boasted the newest computer technology.

"These are all out of commission," the granite-faced man said curtly. "There are 200 computers in here. The master computers are this way."

The orphans followed him to an unobtrusive door on the right. He opened it and gestured for them to go in. Tall, beige metal cases housed the mainframes. Large ceiling fans buzzed insistently, though they couldn't entirely dispel the warmth exuded by the giant computers.

"You have four hours to work on it today," their guide announced. He took up a position by the door, hands clasped behind his back.

Allison licked her lips and sidled up to the closest computer. The rest of the group dispersed around the others. She opened the casing and examined the network of wires and switches. Each was meticulously labeled, and her mind followed them, connected them to their applications, created a picture of the system.

*Everything seems fine. Maybe it's just a short ....*

Allison crouched down and removed plastic façade marked R38. The compartment housed eight circuit boards, which she carefully removed and checked. They all had power. They were all connected properly. As she removed the last one, her hands stilled. Every single chip was missing. She fished out a flashlight from one of her pockets and peered into the compartment. They hadn't fallen off or melted. She sat back on her heels.

"Well? What's the problem?"

The voice was inches from her ear. She whipped her head around and found herself face to face with the government man. His hard blue eyes bored into hers.

"It's really simple, sir," she found herself saying. "This circuit board has been stripped bare. The chips are gone."

"Stripped. They couldn't have fallen off or been knocked off?"

"No, sir. There's no sign of wear or damage to the board. The chips aren't on the compartment floor. Someone removed them."

The man took the circuit board from Allison. Straightening, he scrutinized it with furious intensity. His face hardened in anger. At last he thrust it back into her hands.

"Tell me what you need," he growled.

In a quavering voice she told him exactly what she needed. He scribbled rapidly on a notepad and strode to the next mainframe. There was a low, intense conversation with another orphan in which the man's voice became tighter and quieter. At each successive computer he asked the same questions, was given the same answers: Every station had at least one circuit board missing chips. They had to have been removed by human hands. Rage burned in his eyes, but he did nothing more than very deliberately pocket his notebook and stride quickly from the room. The orphans jumped as the door banged shut behind him. Though muffled, they could still hear the uncharacteristic snap in his voice as he verbally flogged an underling.

Tuning out his rant, Allison contemplated the empty circuit. *What data is on the missing chips? Someone wanted it badly enough to break into a secure building.*

The orphans waited, sweating, for the new chips to arrive. They whispered to each other now and again, nothings about the procedure they'd use to install the new chips and test the system. Allison wiped her face with a rag and tried to control the nausea that threatened to climb up her throat. The heat became oppressive. *If only we could turn off the lights and work in the dark.* The idea of making such a request of the granite government man only strengthened the nausea's grip on her stomach.

He returned abruptly with several cardboard boxes of various computer chips. Setting them down on the floor, he addressed the orphans with his usual steely composure.

"Fix them. Then get out."

He let the door slam behind him.

The orphans scurried to the boxes. They murmured while they helped each other find the right ones. They rapidly plugged in the new chips and reinstalled the circuit boards, calling quick questions and comments to each other. As each finished his job, he gathered his tools and left the room. Allison was next to last, and she waited only a few minutes with the rest of the group in the large workroom.

The army of desks unnerved her. The vast space echoed each rustle and murmur of the group, each sharp command of the guards. They were all enormously relieved when the last orphan emerged, white and harried with his tools cradled to his chest. The guards pushed them and cursed them soundly, so the orphans were quite glad to exit the glass building.

By then it was early afternoon. The sun had no mercy for a bunch of sweaty kids, and most of them turned crimson under its intensity. The walk back to the orphanage was agonizing; the guards refused to let them stop for drinks from public fountains. Allison pushed on wearily, her mind disengaged from her physical discomfort.

*If someone wanted that information, why didn't they hack into the system? Might have been easier. Unless they wanted the GSD to know they'd been there.* Allison swiped at a strand of hair plastered to her forehead. *Oh, none of it makes sense.*

She was almost glad to see the garish flags swaying over the orphanage entrance, and she stepped up her pace just a bit. The entire group welcomed the frigid air of the orphanage lobby with great indrawn breaths. The guards herded them into line to be checked in and took themselves off to the employee section of the building. Allison found herself at the desk just a few minutes later, feeling like an ant about to be squished. Steiner turned an unfocused gaze on her.

"Lean forward," said Steiner mechanically.

"You're done," said Steiner as she tapped a few keys.

"Next," said Steiner without even looking at the queue.

Relieved, Allison savored her walk to the stairs and took her time going up. *What is wrong with Steiner?* She slipped the rubber band from her hair, toying with it as she ascended to her floor. The view from each landing window was an unnaturally darkened picture of summery skies stretched over an architecturally lovely city.

She stopped short at the fourth floor. There wasn't a line for the chamber. The decontamination director and the trim, little nurse were deep in conversation by the inactive doors, so absorbed they didn't notice her.

"All the chips were removed by hand," said the director. Her fingers extended and stabbed the air to emphasize her point.

"No!" the nurse whispered fervently. "They wouldn't dare!"

"Yes, every one of them taken. I'm surprised they didn't destroy the entire mainframe."

"It's so foolish! The GSD have jurisdiction, don't they? I wouldn't like to be on their bad side. They'll probably execute everyone they think is even remotely involved. Oh, this is a terrible blow for the government!"

"Not really," the director smiled at the nurse's frenzied exclamations. "It's not as though that kind of information would influence the public one way or the other. It's really more of a security issue. Heads will roll for this breach, but that's all. I don't think it will cripple our government or damage the Fuhrer in any way. I don't think it will affect the program either. Everything is on schedule, and likely to remain so."

"Well, as long as the schedule is maintained, I suppose we'll be all right. It's only a few months away, isn't it? They never tell me the important dates, but I'm sure you know when the last extermina-"

The nurse caught sight of Allison. Her blue eyes widened, and she grew flustered. The director stiffened, pointed at the decontamination door and glared at the embarrassed girl. Head down, Allison hurried past the grim woman into the chamber. *News travels fast around here.* She hit the button and began counting as the gas destroyed every drop of sweat, every germ she had carried in. *What schedule were they talking about? Extermina-what?* She swayed a little with fatigue and sped up her count so the doors opened at 64.

The hall was astonishingly crowded for this time of day. Jumpsuit-clad orphans flitted from room to room or gathered to buzz quietly about the happenings. Allison stumbled around the clumps of conversation, through the current of wandering kids, to her room.

"Hey, Allison!" A round-faced boy with a loud voice grabbed her shoulder as she was about to step inside. "Have you seen Pete today? Was he working with you?"

"No."

"Well, he better show soon. He owes me his food, and you know I can't get it myself."

"Okay, Sasha," she said wearily.

He sniffed and headed into the room across the hall. A thought dropped into Allison's mind.

"Sasha, wait!"

He pivoted, turned unhappily to face her.

"Pete's rock collection – is it still under his mattress?"

"I dunno. If it is, I'll take it in place of the food. Hey, thanks, Allison!" He smiled widely and went off with a spring to his steps.

*George. Pete. Where are you guys?*

She shook her head to dispel the uneasiness that was beginning to take root in her brain. She turned back to her room and checked herself mid-step, grabbing the doorframe for balance. A lanky newcomer was stretched out on her cot, arms folded across his chest. His unruly brown head swiveled as he took in his surroundings. A glint of metal drew her gaze to his neck; encircling the boy's throat was a thin silver collar, almost as beautiful as the necklaces she had seen in the window of a jewelry store. A tiny red light flared suddenly from it, like an eye opening, glared at her, then winked out. Conscious of Allison's scrutiny, the boy fastened curious green eyes on her. His mouth twisted in a quirky smile, and he raised one hand in a friendly wave.

Allison blinked her surprise. She walked unsteadily to the only empty bed, George's bed, and gulped the half-empty bottle of water Yanna had left for her. When her stomach had settled a little, she slowly ate the bland meal of black bread and cheese. The room was silent. Veiled glances flicked toward the new guy, then spoke soundlessly to each other. Restraint collars were commonly found on adult inferiors, criminals, anyone who was unpredictable or potentially dangerous. The collars had built-in locaters and enough voltage to disable or even kill the wearer. Allison had never seen one on an orphan.

Suddenly the boy got up and wandered over to Roman. He fingered the collar absently as he questioned his nervous roommate.

"Do we have to sleep in these straitjackets or do we get pajamas? ....Why? Like we'd make ropes out of 'em and rappel our way to freedom..... Rappel? It's sorta bouncing down the side of a building, letting rope out as you go...."

Yanna slipped across the aisle to Allison's side. The two girls sat facing each other, heads close together.

"Details," Yanna demanded eagerly. "Let's have 'em."

"It's really weird," Allison said softly. "All the computer chips on certain circuit boards were gone. The government man was really angry. I think they took something really important, but the decon director passed that over...."

"Hold on, you heard *her* talking about it?"

"Yeah. She said the program is still happening, and the nurse said 'extermina-' and then she stopped when she saw me. They didn't want me to know. What do you think, Yanna? What are they doing?"

Yanna pulled at her tangled hair. "I dunno. I hope they weren't talking about us."

"Do you think it had anything to do with George disappearing?".

"Could be a transfer program."

"The only transfer out of here is to the labs. But George was so quiet. He never did anything that would get him in trouble." Allison blanched suddenly. "They wouldn't do that just for fun, would they?"

Yanna shook her head frantically. "Don't talk about that place. I can't think about our friends being tortured for their so-called science."

Her tiny body shuddered. Allison rubbed Yanna's shoulder comfortingly and whispered an apology. The birdlike girl patted her hand and urged her to continue.

"I heard them say BIO and GSD. Do you know what they mean?"

"Bureau for Inferior Orphans."

Allison blinked up at the new boy standing over them. His mouth curved upward, but his eyes shone with something other than humor.

"And the other one?" she asked tentatively.

"Government Security Department. You were in Memory Square today, right? That's where their headquarters is. What building were you in?"

Allison described it, and he nodded.

"Yeah, that's an extension of the GSD. They use it for information storage and program development." He offered a long-fingered hand. "I'm Zip."

"I'm Allison. This is Yanna." She clenched her hands in her lap.

"What kind of a name is Zip?" Yanna asked incredulously.

"All the good ones were taken. I really wanted to be Farley or Nebuchadnezzar or Ambrose. Actually, the tagging system was on 'Z.' You should've seen the director scratch her head. I was gonna be 'Zebra' if I didn't help. So, being the genius I am, I came up with Zip. Brilliant, huh?"

Allison stared at him suspiciously as he hunkered down on the floor beside her bed.

"They just tagged you today?"

"Uh-huh."

"How did they miss you? I mean, they always --"

"Sure they do," Zip grinned. "But I wasn't born in a hospital—slipped through the net. The BIO isn't exactly omniscient."

Yanna caught Allison's eye and moved back to her cot, signaling her distrust of this outsider. Allison hesitated. *He knows a lot about the outside world. Maybe he could....* She met Zip's eyes and read a very familiar expression: calculation. Allison swung her legs to the side of the bed and snatched up the rest of her bread.

"See ya later," she said abruptly as she crossed the aisle to Yanna's bed. Plunking herself down, she resumed eating in silence. Yanna stared at her friend's food, absently winding a curl around her finger. There was a rustle and soft tap of shoes as Zip rose lazily, ambled back to his bed, and stretched out again.

"You guys have issues," he declared to the room in general.

# 3

A llison opened her eyes and stared into the blank gaze of darkness. The walls were still down. Was it the middle of the night? Allison groaned as the dream that had cast her out of sleep possessed her mind again.

*She was tiny, maybe two or three years old, and a beautiful woman held her on her lap. Soft, black hair swept Allison's face, and she giggled uncontrollably. The woman smiled, brown eyes aglow with delight.*

*Crrrrrack, BOOM!*

*The apartment door hit the ground. In poured a sickly red light, in poured men wearing combat gear and black helmets with darkened visors, men carrying guns. Clutching the little girl tightly, the woman jumped to her feet and darted into another room. Allison clung to the woman's shirt, felt the frantic tattoo of her heartbeat. Then they fell. The woman let her shoulder take the impact. She rolled to her back, the girl still hugged to her chest.*

*One of the faceless men loomed over them. Two massive, gloved hands grabbed Allison. She screamed and pushed at him. She called for the woman, but two men held the struggling lady to the ground and tried to gain control of her flailing arms. They managed to turn her over. One knelt on her back, and they clipped her wrists together with a shiny piece of metal. Black hair flowed over her face, but Allison could still hear her gut-wrenching sobs.*

She sat up quickly, drew her knees to her chin. Her whole body shook with the force of the nightmare. *Please go up*, she begged the walls. *Go up!*

Silence.

Allison groped for her blanket, tucked it around her, and rested her forehead on her knees. She measured her breaths and counted them until she came to a number beyond her knowledge. She recited the orphanage rules until memory failed her. She rummaged through her mind for something beautiful and found yellow lilies leaning through wrought iron fence in a public garden. In her mind she traced the smooth, curling petals, peered into the trumpet-like mouths.

Light teased the corners of her eyes, and she raised her head to squint at the darkness receding into the ceiling. Newborn sunlight eased through the window, cast a pallid glow around each bed. Some of the orphans woke to the touch of light and emerged from tangled blankets with sleep-blurred faces. Others, like Yanna, remained imperviously wrapped in their dreams.

Allison rubbed her gritty eyes and wished for the thousandth time that her friend was not such a sound sleeper. Remnants of the dream marched through her brain until she opened her eyes.

Zip strolled past her bed and shot her a quirky smile. It disappeared quickly as he slowed to a halt.

"You look awful. What happened?"

When she didn't answer, he came to sit on her bed.

"What happened?" he asked again, gently.

Allison scrutinized his serious green eyes. No calculation today. Just concern.

"Bad dream," she croaked. "Didn't sleep after it."

"I'll bet you didn't," Zip sympathized.

They watched each other for a minute. Zip's face eased into chagrin as he admitted, "I'm a sleepwalker. You ever do that?"

Allison shook her head slowly.

"Well," he continued, "at home I would sometimes wake up and find myself out of bed, in another room, even outside. Last night I walked into a wall, smashed my nose a bit." Zip tapped the wounded feature tenderly. "Other than that, I slept like a baby. Always liked my room completely dark. Have to congratulate the management on their prime sleeping arrangements. See ya later, Allison."

He sprang up with a mischievous smile and whistled his way from the room. Allison smiled in spite of herself. She pushed her blanket aside, rose and went to wake Yanna. Her friend looked like a human taco with a wild crop of hair sticking out one end. Allison poked until she found Yanna's shoulder, then she shook it hard. Muffled moans and mutters came through the material. Yanna wriggled and peeked out the top of her rolled blanket.

"What?" she demanded groggily.

"Attention!" The loudspeaker trumpeted the Headmaster's morning call. The rest of the sleeping orphans shifted and emerged from their blankets at the gravelly voice.

"Oh, right." Yanna wriggled some more, made it to a sitting position, and yawned. Allison searched for her friend's shoes beneath the bed while they listened to the announcements.

"Groups seven, nineteen, and thirty will not be working today. Remain in your rooms. Groups four, five, twenty-five, twenty-eight, and twenty-nine will report to the lobby immediately after breakfast. The rest remain on standby."

A static click signaled the end of announcements. Yanna pulled a wry face as she scooted to the edge of the bed. Allison nodded in commiseration and handed her the shoes. The wild-haired girl leaned over to put them on.

"I wish we were working together today," came her voice, somewhat muffled by her unruly locks.

"I'm glad I don't have to work today," Allison admitted. "I had a really bad night. The whole dream played out this time, and I couldn't get out of it."

Yanna sat up, her hair swinging back over her shoulders. "Oh, Allison, I'm sorry." She leaned over to give Allison a big hug. Allison closed her eyes and rested her head against Yanna's.

"Have you tried thinking about good things before you sleep?" Yanna asked as she let go.

"Yeah. Doesn't work very well."

"Well, at least you can nap today. Hope your group doesn't get called this afternoon."

"Me, too. Here comes breakfast."

Through the doorway, they caught a glimpse of a tall, metal cart. They joined the others crowding around it and picked up their morning rations of bread, cheese, fruit, and water. The gangly food lady grunted, shouted, and shoved at the kids who reached around her to grab at the food. Allison dodged one of her blows and withdrew with her breakfast to Yanna's bed. The two girls ate quickly, with one eye on the clock above the door. Five minutes left before Yanna's group had to meet.

"Where's the new boy? Zip?" Yanna asked as she craned her neck around.

"He left just after the walls went up. Don't know where he went."

"He's going to starve or land himself in trouble. Just watch."

They munched in silence.

"You think he might be a plant?" Yanna's question jolted Allison's mind.

"No," she answered firmly.

Yanna paused and raised a brow.

Allison crumbled a bit of bread and rolled it slowly between her fingers. "He noticed how tired I am today. He came over and talked with me. He was funny and nice."

"I still don't trust him," was Yanna's verdict. She stuffed bread in her mouth until her cheeks puffed out, then offered Allison her bit of cheese. The bigger girl took it with a nod and waved as her friend jogged out of the room.

A bell sounded from the hall. Allison winced at the vibration driving through her head. Tucking the leftover cheese in a pocket, she got up to go to the bathroom. A few other orphans mingled in the hall to talk away their boredom or simply walk up and down for the exercise. Allison skirted them and turned in the doorway just before the decontamination room.

One yellow light bulb did its best to illuminate the plain gray walls and concrete floor. Two corroded faucets protruded from one wall, and two toilets sat side by side against the opposite wall. A crooked, dirty swath of cloth hanging in front of the toilets served as curtain and hand towel. Sometimes the cloth disappeared for a day, but it always turned up somewhat less grimy.

Faye was there, brushing her teeth and spitting into the drain below a faucet. Her black eyes crinkled in a warm smile. She nodded hello and focused on the drain again, stiff black hair bobbing in rhythm to the toothbrush. Allison rummaged through her pockets for her own toothbrush, turned on the faucet, and added her scrubbing noise to the mix.

The girls finished brushing and headed back to their room together. Faye was silent. To the best of everyone's knowledge, she had never spoken a word since she came to the orphanage. She was a tranquil presence, an excellent listener for anyone in pain or trouble. She seemed to sense Allison's need for comfort and slung an arm around her shoulders. Allison cast a grateful glance at the girl and allowed her serenity to seep into her mind.

"Allison, Faye, come see this!"

Neill had poked his head into the hall, calling to them in a hoarse shout. Faye rolled her eyes as if to say *Silly boys*. Neill withdrew quickly, and the girls followed at a more leisurely pace. Sam and Neill leaned eagerly into the tinted window, but they backed up when the girls arrived.

"What?" Allison asked as she scanned the street below.

"Right there." Sam poked the glass with a blunt finger. "At the corner. He's in trouble already."

Allison pressed her forehead to the window. Zip sat on the sidewalk corner with his forearms resting casually on his knees, unruly head cocked to one side as three guards confronted him. One shouted at the boy and gestured at a work group marching up the street; the other two held their rods casually by their sides. Veins stood out in the speaker's neck, and his face darkened with rage. Zip just sat in a totally relaxed state while the verbal barrage came at him. Allison pictured his lackadaisical grin and held her breath.

"Why didn't he go with the group?" Neill wondered.

"Must be a plant," Sam theorized. "Did something wrong, and they're gonna pound him for it."

"Nah, they wouldn't do that to one of their own spies in public. They'd just take him off secretly, like they did that Ephraim guy. They really want Zip to go to work. What's his game?"

"Gonna get a beating now."

Faye tapped Allison and pointed directly below them. Reinforcements were on the way; four more guards strode toward the scene at the corner. Two red stripes flashed on the leader's sleeve. He stepped between the volatile guard and Zip, forcing his subordinate back a step. The red-faced guard reached around the captain to threaten the boy, and the captain yelled in his face. The junior officer sidestepped the captain and stalked back into the orphanage.

"Holy...." Neill whispered. "He protected Zip."

The captain turned and addressed Zip with his massive arms crossed over his chest. The boy shrugged languidly and got to his feet. The remaining guards gathered loosely around Zip to escort him back into the building.

The orphans drew back and looked at one another.

"He's not a plant," Neill decided, "but he's not one of us. They don't know what to do with him."

"What are you suggesting?" Allison asked blankly.

"Well, he's got protected status, but he's also got that collar. They're watching him, but he's not so valuable that they'd keep him locked away."

"He's a plant all right," Sam said grimly. "They don't beat plants."

Faye shook her head in confusion.

"Well, maybe you can figure it out," Neill said to the group. "All I'm saying is they're making new rules for Zip."

With a curt nod of his head, Sam conceded the point and stumped off to sit on his bed. Faye continued to shake her head as if that might rattle Neill's logic into some kind of recognizable pattern. Allison leaned one shoulder against the wall and shoved her hands in her pockets. She regarded the floor thoughtfully.

"The only thing that makes sense," she mused, "is that they want something from him. And they won't get it the usual way. What do you think, Faye?"

The other girl shrugged, her perfect eyebrows crooked in confusion. She shook her head, her eyes locked intensely on her friend. *Careful*, she mouthed and strode away.

Stunned, Allison followed her progress to her bed.

&ast;        &ast;        &ast;

The ceiling was composed of 52 age-stained squares of Styrofoam.

There were 24 pillars total.

Twelve sagging, mildew-stained beds.

One dismal window.

Allison sighed, turned over again. The nap had refreshed her body, and her mind ticked away like the second-hand on the clock. It refused to pause from its wild conjectures, and so she tried to channel it into counting. Reasonably good idea. Utterly unsuccessful.

At five o'clock, the orphans who had been summoned to work returned. Yanna staggered through the door with a cough, her eyes bloodshot and puffy, and collapsed on her bed. Allison sat up, intent on helping Yanna, when Zip strolled in. As if by silent agreement, the orphans suddenly became very engrossed in their conversations with each other or very sleepy. Zip swung his gaze around the room, whistling cheerfully, and fixed on Allison. She squeezed her hands tightly together.

"Feel any better?" he asked as he approached her.

Yanna turned her head and stared at them. Allison shrugged a mute appeal.

"What?" Zip glanced back and forth between the two girls. "What?"

Allison scrutinized her locked fingers before raising an

impassive face to meet his quizzical stare. Zip shook his head.

"Shunned again," he mourned. "None of you will talk to me. Sam grunts, Neill looks at me suspiciously, and your friend has decided I'm not worthy of her attention." Zip made a mock bow in Yanna's direction and turned innocent eyes on Allison. "Come on, just a little harmless conversation."

He stepped closer and lowered his voice. "I'll tell you anything you want to know."

*Tempting.* Allison listened to the soft buzz of conversation in the room. No one would hear.

"Okay," she whispered, "but use small words."

Zip sprang onto the cot with a cherubic smile.

"Humble of you to admit your lack of intelligence. Ask away."

"What does the GSD do?"

"Oh, those guys are everywhere. Mostly they make sure secret government activities stay secret. Sometimes they act like police: hunting people down, making arrests, and even dispensing justice. They're almost another government in themselves."

Allison frowned. "Aren't there rules they have to follow?"

"Sure, but no one cares anymore. The GSD is the Leader's special pet."

"Who's the Leader?"

"The Fuhrer. The boss. The big man. He runs this continent and a few others," Zip explained patiently. "They put up statues of the most famous leaders all over this city. The bronze guy in Memory Square was the first one. He started the GSD and made it the most powerful agency in the system. It's supposed to protect the government from dangerous people. Mainly orphans like me who escaped their notice."

"How come they didn't know about you?"

"How come they knew about you?" Zip turned the question on her.

"I don't know." Allison chewed a fingernail thoughtfully. "My teacher said they know a little about everyone."

"I thought we orphans weren't good enough for school."

"We have to know about electricity, mechanical stuff, and some English in case we find really old stuff. Machinery or something."

"That's it? Can you write?"

"Just numbers. We're not allowed to write words."

"Makes twisted sense. I went to school until my parents disappeared."

Allison forced back an image of a red-lighted doorway. "How did you survive after that?"

"Stole food sometimes. Someone taught me about phone lines. Last year I helped sell and fix electrical appliances. Illegal, but not a bad job for a minor."

"Is that how they found you?"

"Sort of."

Allison waited for further explanation but none came. She had originally wondered if he ever shut up. *So why don't you brag about avoiding capture? Unless you have something to hide.* Another thought sparked in her mind, and, ignoring caution, she gave voice to it.

"You know something about the break-in at Memory Square."

Zip's expression remained friendly, but his eyes were guarded.

"Intelligent little thing, aren't you," he said slowly.

Allison squirmed and glanced at the clock.

"No comment," he answered finally.

"But you said—"

"I *said* I'd tell you anything you want to know. I never said I'd do it now."

Zip stood and looked at her thoughtfully.

"You're getting bolder, Allison. Be careful."

Allison watched him saunter from the room. Her brain simmered with unanswered questions. He used lots of words she didn't understand, and he had twisted the conversation so he became the interrogator. Emotions swept easily across his face: mirth, loneliness, curiosity, but never fear. Never fear.

# 4

The next afternoon found Yanna comfortably ensconced in Allison's space again with no outward sign of anger or resentment. Allison did notice intense concern in her friend's face and prodded her for answers.

"You can't see how dangerous that guy is," Yanna explained. "I'm worried about you. His collar and behavior could get you in trouble."

"Yanna, he knows so much! I'd go crazy if I didn't have answers to the things going on in my head. The more he talked the more I felt that something isn't right here. I don't see anything dangerous about talking to him about it."

"You've lost your sense. No danger is worth what you want. Leave it alone."

"I can't."

"Can't what?"

The girls were startled to find Zip next to them, hands stuffed casually in his pockets and curiosity in his eyes. The silver collar had taken on a new sheen, and there were traces of moisture on Zip's neck. *Like water. Is he trying to get it off?*

"I can't ignore you," Allison said aloud, glancing at Yanna's bowed head. "Don't sneak up like that. What's wrong with your neck?"

"Nothing," Zip replied a little defensively. "I had some trouble with this primitive and extremely painful device, so I went to visit the nurse."

"Don't you need Steiner's approval first?"

"Come on and I'll tell you about it."

He nodded at the door and spread a very charming smile across his face. She reluctantly left the warmth of her blanket and they wandered into the hall. Yanna's disapproval followed them like a cold breeze, and it took a monumental effort on Allison's part to shake it off. Once she did, she enjoyed how the sunlight filtered through the single window to pick out sparkles in the veined marble. It was relatively quiet then, only a faint buzz of voices to be heard from the other rooms. Zip talked on and on, his voice reverberating pleasantly in the empty corridor.

"So I woke up with a paralyzed neck and went straight to the nurse. She looks just like a doll, doesn't she? That perfect hair and plastic smile. Got the brains of a doll, too."

Allison felt a smile tugging at her mouth and kept her head bowed.

"She asked if I'd seen Steiner, and I told her I was shocked that such an obviously important woman had to have notification from a nominal supervisor. She blushed and stammered very modestly. 'Your medical prowess is positively scintillating,' I said. 'I'm sure you make executive decisions on the basis of your superior status. You're too modest.'

"The woman puffed up like a balloon and declared herself fully capable of handling us pathetic, little orphans without Steiner intruding in her domain. She didn't use the words correctly, but I got the idea. Anyway, off she went with what she thought was a majestic stride...." He mimicked the nurse's mincing step. "....to find some petroleum jelly. I don't remember what else I said, but I was brilliant. Someday I'll be recognized for the genius I am. Until then I'll just have to lavish my dazzling intellect on dolls."

Allison chuckled at his bravado. Zip stopped and clapped both hands to his head in amazement.

"She can laugh! It's a miracle!" He took her hand and patted it reassuringly. "Now don't be scared. It's a perfectly normal reaction to my excellent wit and humor, just a hemorrhage of the funny bone."

Unable to hold back any longer, Allison erupted with laughter. It rang through the hall like a dozen bells. She laughed until her sides hurt and a tiny hiccup escaped her lips. Zip grinned irrepressibly.

"Wonderful job, doctor," he commended himself as he guided Allison to the stairs. "The patient is cured. She's human after all."

"Is that all?" Allison gasped.

"Yep. Laughter is exclusive to the human race. First thing I noticed about this place was the funeral parlor atmosphere. You guys never really laugh."

"We don't have much to laugh about," she said and tried not to hiccup.

They concentrated on getting down the stairs and avoiding a collision. They met only a few passersby, but all of them were in too big a hurry to watch for traffic. All of them fled upstairs. From below them came the echo of boots and the whip-like crack of Steiner's voice. Allison's heart beat painfully. Zip shoved her across the landing and motioned for her to stay out of sight. He hopped down a few steps and sat abruptly. Allison crept a little ways up the next flight and peeked over the edge just as Steiner's head came into view. The woman stomped to a halt and glared at Zip.

"What do you think you're doing?" she barked.

Zip slouched and smiled lazily at her. "I'm out for a walk, a leisurely stroll around the orphanage. Lovely day, isn't it?"

"Shut up and get back upstairs!"

"I like it down here, and you're gonna let me go wherever I want."

Steiner's face turned scarlet and the veins in her forehead popped out. She took a step toward Zip. Her large hands twitched dangerously.

"You see, Steiner," Zip continued conspiratorially, "I know something about you the director would dearly love to hear."

"What?!" Steiner half croaked, half laughed.

"You're a thief. You've been embezzling from this place for years, haven't you? Thought you were safe with the perfect hacking program, but you didn't cover your tracks. While you were snarling at me yesterday, your computer displayed a 'transfer complete' message. Now what is there to transfer around here? Not orphans; the only place they transfer to is the labs, and you wouldn't need to keep that a secret. Not personnel; you're not the one they'd come to for that. The only thing it could possibly be is money. Careless, Steiner. Very careless."

Steiner lunged. Her fist blurred as she swung at Zip's head. He dodged the blow easily and caught her wrist in what appeared to be a loose grip. Steiner jerked her arm back with a cry of pain.

"That was stupid," he said coldly, his face taut with anger. "Stay out of my way, and I might forget about your little transaction. If you call in the BIO, I'll tell them what kind of employee you are."

Steiner rubbed her wrist, her face contorted with rage. She wavered a moment, then retreated with a snarl. Allison waited until her severe bun was out of sight, slipped down the stairs and sat next to Zip. She groped for words until a question finally pushed itself out of her mouth.

"What did you do to her?"

"It's called self-defense. Use whatever means, physical or mental, to protect yourself. It's what I'm best at." Zip paused, a little surprised at his own bitterness, then hopped down the landing to the door. "Come on. I need to see someone."

"Who?" Allison protested as she followed him. "Shouldn't we go back before something else happens?"

Zip held the door for her. "I want you to meet Cuba."

Allison's step slowed when she realized they had entered the giants' dormitories. Instead of a hall she saw only forests of these enormous boys. Her first instinct was to turn tail and run, but her feet seemed to be frozen to the spot. Zip, apparently unconcerned by her reaction, promptly disappeared among the groups of lazy talkers. Someone pushed Allison from behind, and she stumbled into the forest of boys. One olive-skinned giant left off talking when she brushed past, followed her progress with narrowed eyes. Another shouted something derogatory while his group laughed raucously.

Allison swallowed a shout and inched forward. There was little hope that Zip would hear her small cry over the booming conversation and laughter. She twisted her head this way and that, panic rising in her chest, when she ran smack into a wall. She would have fallen if gentle hands hadn't caught her arms to steady her. Allison rubbed her throbbing nose and stared at the myriad buttons and pockets before her. It wasn't a wall but a giant. She tipped her head back, terrified of the expression she would find on his face.

A pair of warm brown eyes met her gaze. His skin was dark brown, and his hair was shaved off instead of cut short. When the boy saw that she wasn't damaged, his face split in a perfect grin and he dropped his hands.

"Stay put, now," he warned in a rich, deep voice. "Little things like you could get squashed in here."

Allison, her mind and tongue suddenly paralyzed, simply nodded her agreement. The giant smiled reassuringly and straightened to his full height. His eyes swept over the crowd and caught on something off to the right. Suddenly his arm shot into the air.

"Hey, dwarf!" he yelled over the din.

Zip's unruly head poked through the human wall just a few seconds later. His puckish face instantly lit up, and he thumped the giant's chest in a friendly fashion. The giant cuffed him gently on the shoulder.

"What're you doing in here, rat?" the big guy teased. "Get sick of trash n' sewers?"

"I came to look after you, you oversized ignoramus," Zip shot back. "No time for pleasantries. I –"

"Why'd you bring this girl? You got no sense. Left her to get trampled."

"Sorry," said a chagrined Zip, "I thought you were right behind me. Allison, this is Cuba, my good friend and my conscience."

Cuba rolled his eyes good-naturedly and engulfed Allison's fingers in a firm handshake. She whispered something polite, then gazed quizzically at Zip.

"I met him a few years ago at a junkyard," Zip explained briefly, then turned back to Cuba. "Something's up," he said in a lower voice. "They pulled me from wire-cutting to infiltrate this place, no reasons given. Just told to look for something fishy. Haven't learned much, just enough to worry me. Not as many work groups going out anymore. What's up with that?"

Cuba's deep brown eyes settled on Allison.

"She's okay," Zip assured him.

"If you're sure." Cuba's square shoulders rose in a shrug. "I don't know what's up, man. We usually work all year, except some holidays and Sundays." He leaned forward a little. "You heard about the disappearances?"

"No. Who's disappearing?"

"We are. Some of my friends go out to work, and they don't come back. That happening on your floors?" he asked suddenly, turning to Allison.

Her eyes widened. "Yeah. Their stuff disappears, too, but I don't think any of us took it."

"Guards take it," Cuba said curtly. "I've seen 'em come in and mess up the beds looking for stuff. If they find anything, they toss it in the trash."

Zip's face went blank. "This is weird. Do you have any idea where the orphans are being taken?"

The giant shook his head. "Nope. There's a pattern to the disappearances, though; it's the oldest ones, and they're separated from their work groups on the way back here. One of the guards just picks a guy out and takes him down a different street. Pretty sneaky."

"Okay," said Zip, "that's a start. Now we need to..."

Allison's mind swam in a fog of the past.

*"It's only a few months away.... when the last extermina-"*

"Extermina-" Allison mused aloud.

Zip's voice froze mid-sentence and he stared at her uncomprehendingly. Cuba bent a sharp gaze on her.

"Say that again," he commanded.

"Extermina...." She quavered under his intensity. "I don't know what the word is."

"You mean 'extermination,'" Zip supplied. "Means 'killing.' Now where'd you hear it?"

"The nurse and the decon director were talking about a break-in at Memory Square. They were wondering if it would mess up some program, and the nurse started to say that word, I think. They stopped talking when they saw me."

The boys looked at each other for the space of a few heartbeats. Cuba folded his arms and looked at her. She got the uncomfortable feeling she was being measured, her words analyzed, her brain penetrated. A genial mask and the giants' lazy way of speaking camouflaged a keen mind.

"Cuba..." Zip started.

"I don't think so," Cuba interrupted. "It's crazy. They need us."

"Maybe. We better find out. Look, I can get into the nurse's office whenever I like. It's a short hop from there to Steiner's office. I'll see what I can find in the system. You buddies with any of the guards?"

"I know one talkative guard, yeah."

"Good. Sound him out. Make casual references to the disappearances, see what he knows."

Cuba nodded once. "Meet you on the sixth floor landing in two days. Noontime."

"Right."

Just then a bell screamed from above their heads, and Allison nearly jumped out of her skin. The giants started to move like an inexorable tide toward the stairwell door. They still talked and laughed and yelled at one another as they went. They pushed at Cuba's back until he stumbled forward. He put an arm around Zip and swept him sideways into Allison. She gritted her teeth as his shoulder pressed her into the cinder block wall. Cuba steered them forward with the flow, broke away from it into one of the dorm rooms. Allison rubbed her sore shoulder.

"Sorry about that," he said with a deprecating smile.

"It's okay."

The last heavy footstep trailed off, and the metal door shut with a firm thump. Allison breathed a silent sigh of relief. *Silence at last.*

"Where are they going?" she wondered out loud.

"Strength training," Zip cut in as Cuba gathered breath to answer her. "And they exercise every muscle but one."

"What's that?"

"Their brains."

"Ha!" Cuba put his hands on his hips. "You want to trade insults, do you?"

Zip raised his hands in a placating gesture. "No, sir, your vocabulary is vast and varied. I will sheathe my tongue."

"Coward." Cuba's eyes gleamed with amusement.

Another buzzer sounded faintly from an upper region.

"I gotta go, you two," Cuba apologized as he led them back to the hall. "We cover everything?"

"Yeah. I'll see you at the landing."

"It was nice meeting you, Allison."

Cuba smiled warmly, one hand extended to her. *I just made friends with a giant.* Allison shook her head mentally, then shook his hand timidly and stepped back for Zip.

"Don't go down any side streets, man."

"I won't." Cuba smiled grimly. "Now get out of here."

The two boys punched each other affectionately. Then Zip took Allison's arm and steered her toward the door. "In case you get lost again," he explained very seriously.

As she went through the door, Allison looked back to see the large boy leaning against the wall. He raised one hand in salute before he turned away.

# 5

Zip was right: the orphanage seemed to be slowing down. Fewer and fewer groups were taken outside, and then only for major jobs. In fact, most of the normal activities ground to a halt. The orphans ate, slept, fought over petty grievances, and milled around their dorms. It wasn't just a change in schedule; there no longer seemed to be any schedule aside from meals and lights out. Allison found the absence of raucous bells slightly bewildering. One change she found quite scary; dorm security had always been invisible something everybody knew existed behind the walls, but now that watchful presence materialized into uniformed men with expressionless faces. They stood motionless as pillars in the corridors while their hawk's eyes darted over the uneasy orphans who dared to venture out of their rooms.

Allison pondered these developments while she twisted a bit of wire into a coil. She gave it one final tweak with the pliers and held it up to inspect her handiwork. It curled like Yanna's hair. She glanced at the huddled form of her friend. Yanna was rolled up in her blanket for a nap. Only a few rebellious strands of hair poked out of her cocoon. Yanna rarely spoke to her anymore, just looked at her out of sad gray eyes. She seemed to be fading away. One day someone might pull back the blankets to find the tiny girl had vanished. Allison blinked back tears and gave the wire a ferocious twist.

"S200017."

Allison's head snapped up. A brown-clothed guard stood in the doorway, hands clasped behind his back, icy blue eyes searching the room. Sam made an incredulous noise, and Allison stared at him. His stolid face shook with fear. He edged off his bed and backed slowly toward the corner of the room. The guard's eyes fastened on him.

"S200017, get your things and come with me."

"I don't have anything," Sam whispered hoarsely.

"Let's go, orphan."

Sam hunched his shoulders together as he forced one foot in front of the other. The granite-jawed guard stepped smoothly to one side as Sam drew up alongside him, then turned to walk slightly behind him. They were gone.

Sam was gone.

Allison's fingers were frozen. She couldn't move her eyes from the doorway. Excited, fearful mutters rose from the other orphans, but her stunned ears couldn't make sense of their language. Faye's weeping gave voice to the pain that welled in Allison's heart.

"R202980!" A harsh voice sounded in the distance.

Zip strolled through the door, hands tucked in his pockets, face pointed over his shoulder. He turned an unreadable expression on Allison as he walked directly up to her.

"I saw Sam," he said tonelessly.

"Yes." Allison's voice sounded foreign to her.

"Got a few minutes?"

Allison looked at the tortured wire in her clenched fingers. She eased them open, let the metal fall to the blanket. "Sure." She stood up stiffly, her limbs feeling heavy and awkward from idleness. Zip tilted his head toward the hall, and Allison followed him there. They edged around the gossiping, anxious groups of orphans, slinked past the decontamination director asleep on a stool by her cleaning chamber, and entered the quiet stairwell. Allison glanced at Zip's bent head as they climbed.

"Are we going to see Cuba?"

"M-hm." Zip's eyes were still focused on his feet.

"Did you find out anything? About what's going on?"

"Yep."

Allison grabbed the metal railing. "What is it?"

"You'll find out in a minute."

She stopped, frustrated. "Who do you work for, Zip?"

He stopped a few steps above her, then turned slightly. "Can't tell you that here."

"Some of the others think you're a plant. A spy."

"Do they now." Zip smiled condescendingly. "What do you think?"

"I don't know! My roommates, my friends are disappearing, and we don't know what's happening to them, and you don't seem to care. You've been nice to me, but you're so hard right now. I don't know what to think," she finished helplessly. Tears welled and burned in her throat.

Zip's smile vanished as she spoke, and he came down to stand beside her. Weariness pulled at his face like gravity and extinguished the humor in his eyes. "Listen, kid, I'm not anybody you should be afraid of. I don't work for the GSD or BIO. I'm not trying to fool around with you. I do care what happens to all of you. I can't tell you anything else. You have to trust me. All right?"

Allison studied his face and his eyes, so tense he seemed to be in pain. *And that's the truth.* She bent her head in acquiescence and covertly brushed at the tears that rushed down her cheeks. "I do trust you."

"Thanks," he said softly. Then he straightened his shoulders and began plodding up again. "Cuba's probably waiting for us."

They found the massive boy leaning on the landing windowsill, eyes fastened on the street below. His expression in the dim light was inscrutable, but it did reveal a jaw clenched so tightly Allison thought it must hurt his teeth. He angled his head to look at them.

"You're late. Everything okay?"

Zip shrugged lazily. "No problems. Got anything for me?"

"Uh-huh." Cuba straightened and faced them squarely. "Half

my floor is gone."

Allison's eyes widened. Zip drew his hands out of his pockets and repeated, "Half."

"There are even fewer of us on the lower levels. Whatever procedure they were using has been changed and sped up. I tried to pump that talkative guard for information, but he shut his mouth tighter than a locked door. So I followed the last kid taken from my room today. The guard hustled him out the back to a military truck. They had all the flaps down. After the kid climbed in, the driver fastened the back with the help of two military types sitting inside. They carried semi-automatics, the blow-your-head-off variety. That's it."

Zip breathed in and muttered to himself. "They're moving faster than I expected." He drew another breath and loosed it quickly. "I got into the computer system. Allison heard right. They're planning to kill off the orphans."

"Why?" Allison blurted out. "They need us, like Cuba said. We earn money for them. We do jobs no one else wants to do. They need us!"

"No, they don't," Zip said quietly, mercilessly. "They created a system to corral all the inferiors in two places: adult camps and so-called orphanages for children. They used you to generate more income for the government. They waited until all the common folk were so used to the idea of you all being interred that they wouldn't miss you if you faded from the background scenery of their lives."

Allison shook her head fiercely.

"No?" Zip's bitter word mocked her. "It's been their plan all along. From the very beginning, from the day their precious Hitler became the Fuhrer. Every country they've ever taken has gone through their purges, and now it's our turn."

Allison covered her mouth with a shaking hand. *Please, no....* She staggered to the flight of stairs leading upward and dropped on the lowest step. She struggled to breathe against the raw pain that clamped around her lungs.

Cuba was silent. The muscles in his face worked and tightened, and his eyes grew hard and remote.

"You... could have broken it to us gently," he said at last.

Zip's face softened. "I'm sorry."

"What kind of animals are they?" Cuba asked in disbelief.

"Hungry ones. And nothing less than the entire world will satisfy their appetite. Maybe when they've finished with it, they'll eat themselves."

"If that's true, you need to get out of here *now*," he told Zip, his voice gravelly with emotion.

"My cover's not blown yet. I think I still have a little time to work out the details. Can you reach the ferry today?"

"Yeah, I've got a job this afternoon."

"Good. Tell her I'm bringing a friend."

Cuba glanced from Zip to Allison. "You can't!" he whispered fiercely. "No orphan's ever gotten out of here! I'm not so sure *you* can do it! Let me bring her out later. I'll think of a way. Please, Zip, they'll track her to the ends of the earth. You know that."

Zip shook his head adamantly. "It's got to be now, with me. The minute I'm gone, they'll sniff around and link her to me. If they haven't already. That conversation she overheard will mean her death. And think, Cuba, think of all she knows about this place! We can use that information to free the rest of the orphans."

Cuba folded his arms and regarded Allison with worry. "You think she could do it? You think you could do it?"

"We have to."

"Man, if you fail...."

"I won't." Zip's eyes grew steely. "I never have."

An anxious silence filled the landing. Cuba broke it at last.

"D'you want to do it, Allison?"

Her eyes focused on his strained face.

"D'you want to go with Zip? You can walk out right now if you want to. I can get you out later. I think."

"But you can't promise," she whispered from behind her fingers.

"No. There's no sure thing."

Allison nodded and retreated into her thoughts. *Get out of here? Maybe. Maybe I could save Yanna and Faye and the others…They'd send us to the labs if they caught us.* She shuddered mentally. *Nothing safe. Nothing sure.* Allison swallowed the bitter taste of fear and made her decision.

"I'll go with Zip." She let her fingers fall to her lap. "I'll try to help."

"Good," Zip said briskly. "We'll leave tonight if we can."

Cuba still stared at Allison, his brows drawn together. "Okay. Anything else you want me to do?"

"Yeah." Zip tapped his silver collar. "Ask the ferry about this thing, will you? Makes me an easy target."

"You bet. Now I gotta go, you two," Cuba said with a glance at the afternoon sun. "I'll meet you at the fifth stairwell this evening, Zip." He turned gentle brown eyes on Allison as she got to her feet. "I'm glad you're getting out, kid, and I hope to see you on the other side." She smiled wanly and whispered a thank you. He inclined his head and strode away, clapping Zip on the shoulder as he passed. "Stay out of trouble, man. Just for a few hours."

Zip smiled his lopsided smile. He turned speculative eyes on Allison.

"Well, if we're gonna get out, we better get a move on." He did an about-face and started down after Cuba.

Allison hurried to catch up, eyes trained on her feet so she wouldn't trip at that hectic pace. "Move? Cuba said we shouldn't do anything."

"No, he said to stay out of trouble. And I fully intend to follow his wise advice. But there are a few things I need to check into or we will have a very unsuccessful escape. How much wire do you have?"

She stumbled a little and reached for the railing. "Wire?"

"How much wire have you got on you?"

"A foot of thick stuff and a few inches of copper."

"Good. Let's slow down. Try to look casual."

"What are you gonna do?"

"We're going to stop at the next landing and have a peek in the door."

His too casual words struck a note of caution in her brain. "What door, Zip?"

"This door." He stopped in front of a brown metal door marked with yellow letters: Caution! High Voltage. Restricted Access.

Allison's blood pressure rose at the sight of those words. "Um, Zip...."

"Wire, please."

She searched through her pockets and gave him what she found. He knelt in front of the door and poked the wire into the ancient-looking lock. It clicked and scraped but didn't open. Several times Zip bent the wire, patiently inserted and twisted it around. The door finally relented with a creak of protest. Zip smiled triumphantly.

"Thank heaven for insufficient funds and good old-fashioned locks. You sit here and keep watch."

"What're you doing?" Allison asked, fearful of his reply.

"Breaking and entering. What's it look like? Rap on the door twice if you hear anyone coming. Then get out of here."

She caught a flash of roguish green eyes before Zip vanished inside. She glanced around nervously as she sat down to wait. *Stay in bed, he says. Don't go wandering around the building 'cause it's getting dangerous. All of a sudden I'm dragged up and downstairs, told all my friends are gonna die, told I'd better leave before I die.*

Her mind conjured images of Yanna and Faye being prodded into the back of a brown military truck. It swallowed them whole. The flaps closed down like the mouth of a giant beast, and it carried them off to an invisible death. Off to satisfy a monster's voracious appetite.

Allison wrapped her arms firmly around her tummy and stared hard at the scuffed tips of her shoes. She listened intently, fiercely, for footsteps, until the silence filled her ears like thick, soft cotton balls.

*I'm guarding a door that screams, "Stay out or we kill you."* She shifted a little on her sore bottom. *The floor might kill me first.*

"Hey," came Zip's hoarse whisper through the cracked door. "Come in here a minute."

*It's like being a pocketknife,* she decided. *Open, shut. Used.*

She climbed stiffly to her feet and slipped through the door into almost total darkness. A small circle of light glowed on the dusty floor at her feet.

"Hold the flashlight under here, will you?" The circle of light skimmed the floor and stopped at the base of a shiny black wall suspended from the ceiling. Allison whipped her head around, squinting, but her vision was blocked by slabs of darkness. So this was where they kept the night.

Allison crouched and took the flashlight from Zip as he lay down on his tummy. He craned his neck to peer at the inch of space between the bottom of the wall and the floor. He flattened his hand and slid it beneath the wall, feeling the bottom delicately. Then he rolled over and sat up to reach for the flashlight.

"Thanks. Go back outside."

Allison stood quickly, turned, and felt blindly in front of her until her fingers stabbed the metal door. She eased through and shut it quietly. She sank to the floor and pulled her knees to her chest. *It's okay. You can breathe. It's fine...*

Daylight guttered and nearly went out before Zip finally emerged, somewhat dusty and nearly giddy with excitement. He pulled her up and hushed her as she opened her mouth. He set a rapid pace down the stairs. The acoustics amplified their footsteps to the magnitude of an elephant's, but no one appeared to yell at them and drag them away. Zip's headlong rush came to a halt at the door to their dorm.

"Keep it natural," he advised Allison as he grasped the handle.

"Zip..."

"Questions later."

He strode confidently through the decontamination area, but Allison's nerves jumped with every step. The childish temptation to run and hide nearly got the better of her when they reached the hall. Most of the remaining orphans clustered in small groups, their voices lowered to murmurs. Their eyes darted and sneaked to the orphanage guards ranged along the walls. Zip and Allison threaded their way among the groups. She looked around her nervously and found Yanna. The wild-haired girl stared at her with pained gray eyes before shifting her focus back to a long-faced boy who spoke in fierce whispers.

Yells erupted from somewhere behind them. Allison looked back in time to see a lanky guard drag an Asian boy into the corridor by his hair, stop abruptly to shake him and kick him in the side. The guards' head swiveled in unison to assess the situation, and several left their posts to gather around the boy and his tormentor.

"Keep up." Zip reached back to grab her wrist.

Allison turned her tear-blurred gaze forward and found she'd caught the attention of one square-jawed guard. His eyes bored into her from the shadow of his cap brim. She dropped her gaze to Zip's heels as they edged around him. The invasive feel of the stare diminished as they entered their deserted room, and the echoes of the scuffle mercifully subsided into memory. Allison released a sigh as Zip led her to his corner to talk. She collapsed on her side and watched him perch restlessly on the next bed.

"We're definitely getting out tonight," Zip announced. "Our cell walls have sensors on the bottom so they stop on contact with the floor. We can fool 'em by covering the sensors before they touch ground. Leave a few feet of space, prop up the wall, and wiggle through. Told you I'm a genius."

Allison was silent. She tucked both hands under her cheek and wondered where to begin.

"What?" Zip asked, sounding slightly annoyed.

*Just say it, I guess.* She asked in a small voice, "Can Yanna come, too? And Faye?"

"No. Are you out of your mind?" He edged forward, leaned

his elbows on his knees, and spoke more gently. "It's got to be just the two of us."

Allison brushed at a strand of hair that fell into her eyes. "I can't leave them here. Who knows when they might be taken, too? How can I just slip out and leave them?"

"We can't take them. Chances of us getting caught are already high, and we don't have anything set up for them on the other side."

Allison rubbed her forehead in a concentrated effort not to cry. "Please, Zip. Please."

"I'm sorry, kid." He touched her forearm gently. "We'll come back for them. I promise."

"Okay," she whispered. "When do we go?"

Zip opened his mouth to reply when two grim watchers strode in. Allison shot up and scooched back against the wall. Her face blanched as they each grabbed one of Zip's arms and half-dragged him away.

"Come on, guys," he complained. "Ease up a bit! I promise to be a good boy."

Then he was gone.

She drew her knees up and tucked her head in her arms.

# 6

L ight scalded her eyes, and she lifted her throbbing head to squint at the window. Late afternoon. She'd been asleep for several hours. Pain shot up her stiff neck as she rubbed her face and swept a few wayward hairs into place. The orphans were all back, lounging in their beds, but Zip was still gone. Allison curled up on her side listlessly.

"Where's the plant?" Neill whispered loudly.

"Gone. Jesse says they took him."

"Huh. He's off to the labs for sure."

Allison sat up suddenly. Neill and Roman were leaning over the aisle between their beds for a chat, but they pulled back and averted their eyes when they saw she heard them.

"So, uh, you hear about the kid who got..."

Allison was on her feet and headed into the hall, so she didn't hear the rest of the sentence. At the same time a guard strode from the opposite door with a white-faced girl in tow. She emitted a squeak as he shifted his grip on her collar and jerked her closer to his side. Her wide hazel eyes touched Allison's briefly. They were glassy with fear. An answering fear thrummed through Allison's veins. *Soon they'll come for me....*

She hesitated.

The guards were still on duty in the hall. How to get past them without drawing their attention?

Sometimes they took several orphans at once, so... Allison trotted to catch up to the guard and his frightened charge and followed closely on their heels. The girl looked over her shoulder once, but the guard shook her ruthlessly for it. Allison bowed her head and watched the tiles glide by under feet.

She entered the stairwell with them and followed them down a couple flights before she slipped away. Soundlessly she opened a door, went through sideways, and inched it shut behind her. Allison exhaled inaudibly. *Made it*, she started to congratulate herself, but stopped cold when she finally looked up.

Guards ranged along the walls, their heads turned toward one in the middle who was telling an amusing story about his sergeant. Five giants stood in a circle not twenty feet away, their impassive eyes fastened on her. For several seconds they regarded each other, then a craggy-faced boy with deep brown eyes broke away from the group. Allison couldn't move. He walked with the lithe, powerful gait of a feral cat she'd seen on the prowl. Allison swallowed as he stopped just a few feet away. If possible, he seemed even larger than Cuba.

"What do you want?" His voice was low, devoid of any emotion.

She struggled to answer. "I'm looking for Cuba. Have you seen him?"

"No."

Those unreadable eyes made her feel even more like a trapped rodent. She twisted her fingers.

"Is he – out on a job?"

"Yes."

"Oh," she whispered, more to herself. "I was hoping."

"Are you Zip's friend?"

She looked up again, startled. "Yes. I'm Allison."

"You'd better go back upstairs."

"But will you tell – " She stopped, puzzled. Something was wrong. It was then she heard, beneath the loud-voiced guard, the deep reservoirs of silence that surrounded them. *Where are the other giants? They can't all be working.*

She continued, her voice calmer than she felt. "Will you tell Cuba I came here? That they took Zip?"

He nodded.

Allison's face began to crumple. "I just don't know what to do."

"Go on back up," the giant said almost gently. "I'll tell him. If he comes back."

Allison could take no more. She reached blindly for the door handle, yanked it, and edged through. She returned to her dorm blinded by unshed tears and unable to remember how she'd made it past the watchers. Neill and Roman chatted nervously together. Yanna had shifted to lie on her stomach, her face concealed by a fall of curly hair. Faye was nowhere to be seen. Allison stumbled to her bed and sat down heavily.

*What now?* she begged nobody in particular. *What can I do now?*

She slid her hands over her mouth to clamp down the despair that threatened to burst forth in sobs. But she couldn't stop the tears that coursed over her fingers. She cried for herself, for Zip, for the orphans who waited for death to come and claim them.

*          *          *

"Hey, you'd think we'd get more food with everyone getting transferred out of here," Neill complained. He scowled at the departing matron and her empty food cart as he and Roman returned to their beds with their dinner.

"Only you would think that," Roman replied. "Everyone else knows they'd never do something so nice for us." He paused. "You really think we're all being transferred?"

"Sure."

"Why?"

"Well, what else would they be doing?"

Roman shrugged and took a bite of hard cheese as he thought it over. "Seems pretty sneaky for a simple transfer."

Allison glanced sharply at Roman. He was so close to the truth. Should she tell them all what was really going on? She hugged her arms tighter over her tummy and lowered her head again. It wouldn't make any difference. They still wouldn't have any chance to escape what was coming. No, it would only induce a state of panic.

She felt so tired. All her bones wanted to sink into the thin mattress, but she made herself stay upright until lights out time. So tired, and yet she dreaded sleep. The old nightmares were sure to prey on her mind while she was in this emotionally fragile state. Allison looked up at the window, at the soothing twilight that hushed the sun to sleep. Not much longer anyway.

She started to stretch out for sleep when two guards hauled a limp Zip in by the arms. They dumped him unceremoniously on the empty bed next to her and stalked off again. Allison stifled a cry and scooted across the aisle to kneel beside him. Zip was a mess. A black eye, colorful bruises, and a split lip <u>left rendered</u> him almost unrecognizable. He struggled to a sitting position, winced and hugged his ribs. Allison started to tear up a frayed blanket for bandages.

"I thought you were gone for good," she whispered tearfully.

"Not quite," Zip rasped.

"What did they want?"

"I hate being right, but the GSD goons are onto something. They wanted names, locations, meeting times."

"Huh?"

"I'm part of a resistance group. Couldn't tell you that earlier, but I think my cover's blown now, don't you?"

Allison paused to stare at him. "Resistance?"

"Yeah, we resist, or should I say fight against, the GSD. Anyway I didn't talk, so they got rough. Fancy drugs have nothing on good, old-fashioned torture." Zip paused to unbutton his jumpsuit so Allison could wind the bandages around his ribs. "Their weakness is pride. They underrate us inferiors both physically and intellectually. It doesn't occur to them to look beyond us for other 'criminals.' Watch it! I happen to enjoy breathing. When we get out of here our ferry will be a superior girl. So much for their lofty theories."

"Ferry?"

"Contact, guide. She'll take us to safe houses. We'll be in hiding for a while –"

"You talk a lot for someone who just got beat up."

Zip attempted to smile and thought better of it. "Okay, then. Watch for three sensors underneath the wall as it comes down, the one that blocks off the aisle. They're about a foot apart. An alarm will go off if you don't cover all three at once."

"Can't we just get out before the wall comes down?"

"Not without being caught by the goons. They seem to like casting shadows through doorways. I'll bet they don't leave until everything is shut down. There's a weird echo after these walls hit, and I think it's another that blocks off the doorway. No, we have to fool the sensors and wait a minute for that last wall."

"Fool them with what?"

"Maybe part of the bed. That's what I'm gonna do."

A bell clanged, and a watcher bellowed from the doorway. Zip gestured for Allison to get back to her bed. She slipped back and perused the sturdy-looking bed frame. With a hasty glance over her shoulder, Allison grabbed the frame and tugged experimentally. It was like trying to move a brick wall. She lay flat on the floor and poked her head underneath. Four wooden boards supported the thin mattress, and they appeared to be movable. She sat up, caught Zip's eye, and touched one of the boards.

.   The room plunged into semi-darkness before he could respond. Allison scrambled onto her bed, hands shaking as she emptied her bulkier pockets. Guilt assailed her as she remembered Yanna and Faye. *You'll be okay. I'll help get you out before they take you away.* She curled up on her side.

A watcher's shadow filled the door as familiar whirring sounded through the ceiling. The black walls slid down at a sluggish pace that nearly drove Allison mad. She waited for them to cut off the shadow's waist before rolling to the floor. She grasped underneath the bed, wrenched a board free, and crawled to the edge of her cell. She turned on her back and held the board like a shield against the oncoming wall. Three sensors sparkled in it like cut glass. Allison repositioned the board. At the first sense of pressure she squeezed her eyes shut.

It stopped.

A muffled thump caused her eyes to open. It was only the black slab that sealed off the door. Something rustled near her head. She stared up at Zip's dim outline.

"You can come out now," he whispered, slightly amused.

She squirmed out carefully and let Zip take over. He propped the board up with another and turned to the window, dusting his hands. Allison rose shakily to join him. There was just enough light from the street lamps to cast Zip's swollen features in eerie shadows. He tilted his head and smiled ghoulishly at her. The silver collar was noticeably absent.

"You got it off?" Allison asked quietly.

"Took some tweaking, but it really wasn't a smart design. Watch out for the tools."

Allison stepped away from the dark lump at her feet.

"We're going through the window? What about the alarms?"

"They'll only go off if you break the glass. Hold this, but don't touch the tip. It's sticky."

She gripped the small rod Zip thrust at her. He talked softly as he drew a pencil-thin tool along the outside of the casing. Zip pocketed the instrument and took the rod back from Allison. He set the wide, round tip against one side of the casing and pushed hard. The window slid out and a little to the right with a small squeak. Only the alarm wires held it in place. Zip bent to pick up a pair pliers and jerked upright with a grunt.

"Allison, can you grab those for me? Thanks."

He judiciously snipped ground wires along one side and the bottom. Allison stood on tip-toe to reach the ones at the top. The window was now perfectly positioned for them to squeeze through sideways. He instructed Allison to pick up a sharp T-shaped peg and a hammer.

"Now lean out carefully and drive it into the wall."

Allison angled her body between the wires and pretended they were red hot to keep herself from touching them. She placed the peg against the cinder block wall. It shook terribly. She took a deep breath of clear night air and tightened her grasp. Repositioning the peg so the sharp tip nestled in a groove of mortar, she began to tap at the top.

"Harder," came Zip's hoarse voice.

She poured every ounce of her fear into her efforts until each blow of the hammer rang like a trumpet in the stillness. Crumbs of mortar fell like rain to the street below. When half of the peg was buried in the wall, Allison eased her upper body back inside. Zip produced a makeshift rope of blankets tied together and fed one end out the window to tie around the peg. Allison bit her lip and folded her arms across her aching torso. *I guess now is a bad time to tell him I'm afraid of heights.* Zip was too busy tying off the rope to notice her anxiety. Once finished, he lowered the rest of his makeshift rope down.

"Okay," he finally whispered. "Just go as slow as you want and keep your eyes on the wall. Or keep them closed. I'll go first."

He pressed her arm reassuringly and climbed carefully through the gap. As soon as his head disappeared, she sat on the edge and slid her legs through. *Deep breaths. Don't look down.* Awkwardly she grabbed the window ledge and lowered herself until the peg was eye-level. Her arms shook badly. She locked her gaze on the gray wall, clenched her teeth, and grabbed the rope with her right hand. The fingers of her left hand lost their grip on the ledge. She caught at the rope as she began to fall and got it with both hands.

"Ohhh!"

"Allison!" Zip whispered fiercely. "You okay?"

"Yeah," she managed. *I'm dangling over a concrete sidewalk four stories below me. I'm fine.*

"Just take it easy. I'm about fifteen feet below you. I'll hold the rope for you when I get to the ground."

"Okay."

Her biceps trembled as she pulled herself up and curled her legs around the rope. With a deep breath she began to lower herself down. The new skin on her palms burned each time she shifted her grip on the rope. *Just a little ways to go,* she encouraged herself, *so ignore it*. It was a nightmare of blank walls and intermittent windows that seemed to glare at her, even in their blindness. She winced each time her foot or knee banged glass, sure the unusual noise would attract someone's attention. At last she felt Zip touch her shoe, and she dropped like a stone to the ground.

Their hands found each other in the dark, and Zip pulled her to her feet. She gritted her teeth against the burn of the contact on her chafed skin. Zip raised a finger to his lips and, keeping one of her hands tightly in his, they weaved through the shadows around the yellow street lights. They played this game with the lights for several blocks. Then, with a sharp-eyed glance around the area, Zip struck out across the street toward an alley.

He led her deep into a network of the unlighted little streets, and they turned this way and that until Allison felt she was spinning in circles. When one alley opened into a street, Zip stopped and poked his head out like a turtle. They waited tensely for an idle taxi or pedestrian to move on before they emerged from their lightless hole to slink across the open pavement into another lightless hole. Allison threw her head back and sucked in the night air. A few stars glowed feebly above the light-polluted city. They blurred together and snuffed out as she blinked and lowered her eyes to the gloom of the back streets. Zip was black smudge of movement, a bony grip around her fingers.

"Keep it up," he threw back over his shoulder. "We're doing fine!"

*No, we're not.*

Allison's untrained legs gave out, and she crumpled into an oily puddle. Every breath tortured her lungs. Zip picked her up again and urged her on. She ran drunkenly for another block before she careened into the moist brick wall of a hardware store and lay where she fell. Her body wanted to melt into the unforgiving ground, and she was inclined to allow it.

"Come on," Zip wheezed. He bent over her with a hand to his ribs. "There's no time to rest."

She pushed her body off the cement and staggered alongside him. He kept her walking at a snail's pace for a few minutes before he let her sit down on the cracked stoop of a decrepit bakery.

"Let's get you some water," he said sympathetically.

They ventured out to the sidewalk of a dilapidated residential district. Tufts of weeds sprouted in the yards of the slouching houses, and light leaked around their haphazardly curtained windows. In a neglected public park he found a leaky water fountain for her, and she sucked at the precious drops until she gagged. Their thirst appeased, they stole back into the anonymous alleys.

It was then they heard another set of footsteps behind them. Zip dove into a tiny alley, dragged Allison with him, and they waited apprehensively for the person to pass by. His feet pounded the sidewalk like kettle drums, and his rhythmic breathing sounded unnaturally loud. Allison gulped down a sob of fear. Zip squeezed her hand encouragingly.

The runner shot past their hiding place without so much as a hitch in his stride, his sweatshirt hood bobbing against his narrow back. Zip leaned out cautiously to watch him go, then led Allison out to the street again. They stepped into a clumsy jog. Zip didn't complain about his ribs, but his breathing was sharp and forced. He watched Allison's condition closely for a few blocks. When she tripped over her own shoes, he helped her up and set the pace back to a walk.

"Is it far now?" Allison croaked.

"Just a couple blocks. Here, you put your arm around my shoulders, and I'll help you."

He slid a wiry arm around her waist and gripped her ribs.

"What about your injuries?" Allison protested, her arm hovering over his back.

"I'm fine," he said shortly. "Now let's go."

She settled her hand lightly on his shoulder, and he half-dragged, half-carried her.

It was still dark when they hobbled up to a junkyard in a dingy neighborhood. Zip lowered Allison to the concrete sidewalk, and she rested her head against the chain-link fence.

Her feet were on fire. Pain gripped her calves and thighs, shot up into her sides and tore at her lungs. She heaved the burning air in and out. Zip looked tensely around the deserted street. All was quiet and still.

Zip drew in a ragged breath and whistled a few bars of a song. An answering whistle echoed weirdly in the night, and two figures emerged a block away. As they came closer Allison was surprised to see that they were women, one middle-aged and one much younger. They each shook hands with Zip and exchanged a few quiet sentences. Allison's heavy eyes were getting the better of her when someone laid a warm hand on her shoulder. Zip's eyes glittered as he crouched next to her.

"I have to go now," he said gently. "I'm sorry I had to push you like that. Don't worry about anything, okay? I'll be in touch."

She nodded drowsily and watched him disappear down the street with the older woman. A pair of soft, strong arms helped her up and supported her around the waist.

"I'm afraid you'll have to walk two more blocks," a voice murmured apologetically. "You can sleep in my car, all right? Just stay with me a few more minutes."

Allison blinked away the encroaching sleep and clumsily set one foot in front of the other. The two girls swayed the last few steps to a compact car in a grocery store lot. Whispering encouragement, the stranger propped Allison against the car and opened the back door. She helped the exhausted orphan crawl inside and watched her collapse in a stupor. Dreams of distorted alleys flitted lightly through Allison's mind, and a sensation of weightlessness carried her away.

# 7

A mouth-watering aroma enticed Allison from sleep and prompted  memories of a bakery that displayed its freshly-baked donuts outside to attract passersby. Her stomach gurgled in anticipation. She cracked an eyelid but forgot about food when the room came into focus. Soft peach walls melted in the morning light, a perfect backdrop for the creamy white furniture. Pictures, stuffed animals, and piles of clothes made a pleasant, girlish clutter. A breeze stirred the curtains at the window and brought with it hints of bird songs and distant car motors. Allison burrowed in the covers and groaned. Her body was one massive lump of pain, but she drifted off again anyway.

She woke feeling like there was there was something she was supposed to do, something she had missed. Confused, she craned her head for a look around. There were the peach walls instead of gray concrete. *No more black walls, no more guards. This is weird. Beautiful, but weird.*

Footsteps sounded outside the door, and someone fumbled with the knob until it clicked open. A tray of steaming food came through followed by a tall girl with extremely fair skin and a mane of blonde hair. She looked like an old-fashioned doll with her delicate, flower-like face. Her blue eyes lit up when she saw Allison was awake. She set the tray on the nightstand and perched lightly on the edge of the bed.

"Hi! How're you feeling?" she asked sweetly.

Allison brushed at her hair and sat up gingerly.

"Awful."

The girl laughed musically. "Yeah, that was a dumb question. I'm Analiese, Lee for short. I heard Brandon was bringing a friend, but he didn't mention your name."

"It's Allison."

"Allison," Lee repeated carefully. "That's pretty."

"Where's Zip?"

"Is that what Brandon called himself at the orphanage? Sounds like something he'd pick. Well, Zip is with friends. Don't worry about him; he's always okay. You're the one everybody's concerned about. May I look at your feet?"

Slightly embarrassed, Allison only nodded. Lee stood and peeled back the covers at the foot of the bed. She frowned and tossed her hair over one shoulder as she bent down for a closer examination. Through the constant throbbing Allison felt a touch so light it almost tickled.

"We'll have to soak 'em," Lee announced, "But they'll be just fine in a few days."

She straightened and looked critically at Allison.

"That thing you're wearing has got to come off. It should be burned. How long have you been wearing it?"

Allison stared down at her dingy outfit. "Ever since I can remember," she confessed, "we've always worn the same thing."

Lee's eyebrows shot up.

"Not the *same* jumpsuit," Allison said weakly. "I mean, when we grew out of one, they'd give us another bigger one."

Lee said something under her breath. Shaking her head, she began to gather various things from a white-doored closet set into the wall at the foot of the bed and a tall oak dresser. Allison followed her movements closely, curiously examining her two-piece outfit with the skirt that swished around her knees. The girl's long-fingered hands scooped and gathered and sifted. She moved with a liquid grace, and her presence had a pleasantly busy air. *She seems all right,* Allison mused to herself, *just a little strange. But maybe that's normal out here.* She relaxed a little more.

Lee straightened beaming from a drawer and crossed to the bed to dump her findings on the coverlet. Sifting through the pile, she held up a soft brown skirt and a creamy ivory blouse. Allison's eyes widened.

"What's wrong?" Lee asked, her smile wilting.

"I can't wear those."

Lee lowered her arms. Then her face cleared, and she nodded.

"I understand. Too much change too quickly. Well, you can try some of these other things. They might be too big, but we can roll them up or cut them off. Just try on whatever you like."

She stepped back a little, delighted, as Allison tentatively touched a pair of flannel pajamas pants.

"They're really soft," she murmured.

"Here, I'll help you with them. Think you can stand up for a minute?" She froze with a strange expression on her face. "Hang on . . . . What are you wearing under that?"

Allison stared up at Lee, her fingers motionless on the top button of her jumpsuit. "You wear more clothes underneath?"

The next few minutes following Lee's whirlwind search for her "old things" caused Allison a great deal of embarrassment, but she eventually found herself swathed in soft blue pajamas. Lee overrode her protests against shortening the pants with a careless wave of her scissors.

"I can easily buy more clothes," she argued, "whereas you are not allowed to show yourself outside for a while."

Allison closed her mouth and let Lee have her way. The blonde-haired girl settled her guest on the bed, flitted from the room, and returned with a sand-colored towel draped over her shoulder and a metal basin in her hands.

Allison leaned her shoulder against the headboard and dipped her feet into warm, soapy water while Lee flitted off again. Allison winced as the soap worked into a broken blister. All sensations of pain ceased when Lee entered with a tray of steaming hot food. Allison balanced a plate of pancakes on her lap and took small bites, rolling the sweet bread on her tongue until she absolutely had to swallow. Lee encouraged her to ask about anything as she bustled around the room and shoved her messy piles out of sight.

"Anyone else live here?" Allison ventured.

"Oh, sure," Lee replied breezily. "My parents are having breakfast in the kitchen right now. They're just really quiet in the morning. Actually Dad should've left for work, but you can meet my mom. She's anxious to know if you like her cooking."

"Is she like you?"

"We look alike, but she's shorter and not so talkative. Blue eyes and light hair run in the family. You're so lucky to have a perpetual tan. I always burn when I lie out in the sun."

"Per-pet . . . .?"

"I'm sorry. I meant you're skin color doesn't change. I have to go help my mom now, but I'll check on you every now and again. Sound good?"

"Yeah." Allison fumbled with her fork for a minute. "What should I do?"

Lee chuckled. "Nothing. Relax and heal. I'll be back soon."

She gathered the breakfast dishes and sailed from the room. Allison dried her feet gingerly with a towel and eased back under the covers. Lee made her feel safe and peaceful, though it was sometimes disconcerting to look into those steady blue eyes. They didn't measure like Cuba's, but they probed at her. Allison's eyelids began to droop....

A faint scuffle interrupted her doze. She sat up and pulled the sheets around her protectively. Her blood began pounding when she remembered the sounds rats made. The scuffling noise was replaced by a low thrum. A bundle of fur shot onto the bed with a throaty squeak. Allison jerked away from it and banged her head on the wall.

The low thrum resumed as the creature twitched its tail and gazed at her out of round yellow eyes. It rubbed its cheek against her leg, kneaded the covers with its forepaws, and plopped down in an undignified position. Allison's heart slowed. It was a cat.

Most of the cats she had seen were feral or strays that hissed and ran when people approached them. This one just lay there, belly up, and rumbled. She reached out cautiously to touch its fur. The cat purred louder and squeezed its eyes shut with pleasure. Allison stroked its chocolate-striped fur and found she enjoyed the silky feel. When her fingers wandered up its chest, the cat gripped her hand and sampled her skin with its tongue. She smiled.

Suddenly the cat rolled over, ears swiveling forward. Allison looked up to see an older version of Lee leaning against the door frame. Her oversized shirt was dusted with flour, and her hair was pulled back into a messy bun that left wisps floating by her cheeks. A smile spread across the woman's face, and humor twinkled in eyes that could have been Lee's.

"I see you've met Coffee," she commented. "We missed him at breakfast. Is he behaving himself?"

"Yeah, he's really nice." Allison glanced down shyly.

"I'm Regina Krueger. And your name is Allison, right?"

"Uh-huh."

"Welcome to our home. We're planning to have you stay for as long as you want." She paused. The laugh lines disappeared. "Lee said you came from an orphanage. You might find our world somewhat confusing and scary, so please let us know if you're uncomfortable about anything. We won't be able to completely understand, but we want to help in any way we can."

Tears pricked Allison's eyes. Mrs. Krueger sensed her loss of control and moved toward the bed.

"I'm sorry," she said quietly as she extended her arms to hug Allison. Allison involuntarily shrank away from her touch. Regina stepped back awkwardly, her face tight with emotion. She stepped to the side, scooped up Coffee, and sat down in his place.

"It's okay," Allison said finally. "Thank you. For the food and for letting me stay here.

"You're welcome." Regina smiled and stroked Coffee's striped head. "Lee said you've only been awake for an hour. Are you still pretty tired?"

"Yeah."

"Anything I can get you?"

"No."

"Well, I'll be around. Call me if you need me."

Allison nodded.

Regina looked down at the cat stretched out in her lap.

She shifted to stand up, and Coffee came to curl up by the pillow. He tucked his face under one paw and went back to sleep. Allison watched drowsily as her hostess pulled the curtains across the window and picked up the breakfast tray.

"Sleep well," Regina said gently as she left the room.

Allison's heart constricted at the pain she'd caused. *I'm sorry. I want to trust you. I do.*

# 8

It was getting into the wee hours of the morning, and the Director of the Government Security Department still sat at his desk. He spread his fingers over the glossy, dark wood and took a long breath through his nose. Between his hands lay a plain manila folder that contained a report from the head of the BIO. A very disturbing report. His face twitched as he contemplated the situation.

Two orphans had escaped, one of them an important link in the chain of resistance. They hadn't bothered to try covering up their disappearance. That makeshift rope dangling out a window for everybody to see—it was a taunt. A challenge. His best men were combing the city, but no one had seen them. The brats had shrewdly avoided public places.

The GSD had the most intricate network of information in the government; the Director knew every sordid detail of every official's life, every crime committed in the alleys of the smallest towns, every birth and death in the Reich. Yet he could not find two half-grown inferiors wandering around the streets of the capitol city. His city.

He seethed with fury.

The brass desk clock ticked softly, and the Director stroked the desk with one fingertip in time to its soothing beat. Time was on his side. It was a small advantage, but he could afford to be patient. He could wait for the resistance to move, as they would eventually be forced to do.

As he stared at the report, an idea bloomed in his consciousness. The Director picked up his phone and punched a number. His secretary answered with a groggy murmur.

"Sir?"

"Call my wife at some decent hour. Tell her I'll be staying at the office for a few days."

"Yes, sir."

"And get Gunther for me."

"Now, sir?"

"Did I say tomorrow? Of course *now*!" The Director smashed the phone back in its cradle.

If this worked, and he knew it would, he could snare the rest of the traitors hiding in this city. Perhaps even find Papa and break the chain of resistance across the country. His lips curved upward in a cold smile.

# 9

Allison drifted in and out of sleep over the next 24 hours. Sometimes Regina Krueger was there, reading a book by the window, humming softly as she folded Lee's clothes, or simply watching her out of serene blue eyes. Allison woke finally to the muffled thump of a car door and the deeper tones of a man's voice weaving through the flutelike voices of the women. Dusky light filtered through the curtains with the first verses of cricket songs. Allison nervously scooched up to lean against the headboard. She brushed the last traces of sleep from her eyes as the voices moved through the house and wound their way to her door.

"Come in," she replied tentatively to their soft knock.

Regina came in first, leading a thin man in a dark blue suit and loosened tie. He smiled warmly as soon as he saw Allison, and his kindness brightened his tired features.

"Hello, Allison," came his smooth baritone. "I'm Sean Krueger. Congratulations on your escape—the first successful one in history."

Brown eyes twinkled at her behind scholarly glasses as he shook her hand. Allison's mouth curved upward in an answering smile. Warmth radiated from this small man and soothed her nervousness. She relaxed against the headboard as Regina and Sean settled in chairs and Lee perched on the bed with her.

Mr. Krueger leaned back in the desk chair as he cleaned his glasses. Tiny lines traced the corners of his eyes and edged his mouth.

"Well, Allison," he said, "I'm glad you're recovering so quickly after such a rough night. It really was the perfect escape. The police and the GSD have been searching high and low and found no sign of your route."

Allison nodded.

"There are bulletins in the newspapers and alerts on the radio warning the city folk to watch for you. So, while we would love to give you total freedom, we must ask you not to stand close to the windows or venture outside. We must wait a little until the initial frenzy of the search subsides. All right?"

"Yes," Allison choked out through a throat that had suddenly gone dry.

Sean Krueger put his glasses on and folded his hands comfortably. "Don't be frightened by the fuss. We have experience on our side. Regina and I have sheltered many, many fugitives and watched as the GSD tore apart the city to find them. All our guests have made it to safety."

Allison twisted the covers in her fingers. "Can I ask a question?"

"Sure."

"Why did you take me in?"

Mr. Krueger leaned forward, studying her with keen eyes.

"We believe that no one is superior to anyone else. The BIO has no right to treat you like dirt because you are just as human as they are. They're a powerful group in high favor with the Leader and the ordinary citizens, so we can't openly protest their actions. Anyone who expresses opinions contrary to those held by the government is jailed or executed. You see, there are very few of us. If we are stamped out, there will be no one left to oppose the BIO and help those under their persecution. The best thing we can do to oppose them is deprive them of their victims. The best way we can help you is to remain secret."

Allison nodded. "Can I ask another question?"

"Sure," Sean Krueger smiled gently.

"What will happen to me now?"

"Until it's quiet enough to move you to a safer country, we have permission to take care of you. Is that all right with you?"

Allison nodded again. "And my friends? Zip promised you

would help them."

"Yes." Sean leaned back. "That is our plan. The leader of our group is coming to interview you tomorrow evening. Whatever you can tell him about the orphanage system and what you've seen and heard about this... extermination plot will help your friends. We've been trying to get you all out for years, but we've never had an opportunity until now."

Allison couldn't stop the tears racing down her cheeks or the harsh sobs that shook her entire body. Lee slid over and held her as years of pain and all her recent fears poured out. All that time in the darkness, someone had been trying to free her. These people had put themselves in danger to save her and her friends. *Why? Why?* Allison brushed at the watery haze that ruined her vision and nearly choked on a hiccup. She smiled weakly into Lee's clear eyes, eyes that reflected her misery and relief.

"May we join in?" Regina asked with a teary smile.

"Yeah," Allison croaked.

Regina and Sean came over to embrace her gently. Allison leaned her head on them and breathing in their scents of flowers and shaving cream. A peaceful sense of security flooded her heart, something she hadn't felt since early childhood. Memory clouded the present with an image of a dark-haired woman who held her close after a fall on the kitchen floor. Someone pressed a wad of tissues into her hands as she started to sniffle again. Regina knelt in front of her and tenderly brushed the hair away from Allison's forehead.

"Time to rest and heal," she said tenderly.

Actually it's time for everyone to rest," Lee yawned. "How long have we been talking?"

"Well," Sean arched an eyebrow at his daughter. "I didn't hear you talking, but I thought I might have heard a few snores during the conversation."

"Ha!" Lee stood and poked him in the chest. "*You* weren't up at five this morning, were you."

Sean stroked her hair affectionately. "No. Off to bed with you, my hard worker."

Allison's throat contracted. "You're leaving me alone?"

They all turned sharply at the dread in her voice.

"We thought you'd prefer that," Regina explained. "Would you rather have Lee stay in here with you?"

"Yes, please," Allison answered softly.

"Well, Lee," Sean said thoughtfully, "let's find that folding cot for you. I think there's plenty of space for it in here."

"We can make space," Lee suggested as she headed for the hall.

"I'm not up for moving all that furniture around again...."

They returned with a twin-size mattress, and Regina burst into gales of laughter when it stubbornly refused to round the hall corner and wedged itself halfway into the room. Sean made several dry remarks about the paralyzing effects of laughter before his wife was able to come to their rescue. One last heave carried it through and nearly sent them all tumbling to the floor. Sean and Lee positioned it perpendicular to the bed while Regina went in search of a pillow, sheets, and blankets.

*They behave like children.* Allison smiled to herself and enjoyed how the little family teased each other as they worked. Finally the portable bed was made and Lee slipped under the covers with her head close to Allison's bed. Allison couldn't suppress a shudder when Sean turned the light off. The Kruegers hugged their daughter goodnight, whispered their love and wishes for a good sleep. Then they came to Allison's bed.

"Good night, Allison," Sean embraced her very gently.

"Sleep well, honey," Regina whispered on her turn. "You're safe now."

The door closed soundlessly behind them. Allison turned on her side and tucked the blanket tightly under her chin. *Don't be afraid,* she told herself, focusing on the streetlight glow that peeked around the curtains.

"It was good to see you smile," Lee commented as she rustled comfortably under the covers.

"It does feel good," Allison answered.

"The orphanage system didn't give you the chance to be a child, did it?"

"No.".

"Were you close to the other kids?"

"Yeah. My best friend was Yanna. We came to the orphanage

at the same time."

"She couldn't come out with you?"

"No." Allison's throat closed.

"I'm sorry. But I'm glad you got out. I've never met anyone like you, and I'm probably going to drive you crazy with my questions."

Allison was unable to stifle her yawn.

Lee chuckled. "Or maybe just bore you. I'll let you sleep now. Night, Allison."

"Night."

# 10

**F**rantic knocks beat a tattoo through Allison's dreams. She jerked upright, expecting to see that hideous red light from her nightmare. No, only a small slice of yellow light peeked in underneath it. The drumming stopped abruptly, and low, urgent voices floated from the hall. Lee stumbled from her bed and wrapped a robe around her disheveled pajamas. Glancing back at Allison, she slipped out and closed the door silently behind her.

*Maybe it's Zip,* Allison thought to herself. She wriggled from her tangled sheets and staggered into the brightly lit hall. Allison followed the hall until it opened into a foyer and living room. Sean stood directly in her line of vision with his back to her, barely five feet away. Backing up, Allison sat down to listen.

"He'll need new clothes," Regina said.

"Are you sure you weren't followed? Lee, bring them some water."

"We lost them a couple miles back," a stranger replied gruffly. "I don't think they'll trace us here, but we'll be off shortly anyway. He has to get out of the city tonight or he'll miss the rendezvous."

"How did they know?"

"There must be a leak. We kept him under wraps, told only a few about his location. There's no other explanation for it."

The clink of glass followed a husky "thank you." Someone paced the floor with heavy, impatient strides. Allison crawled forward, peeked around the corner. Sean shifted his weight a little, revealing a tall, stocky man stretched out on the couch, exhausted. He balanced a glass of water on his shabbily clad chest and brushed shaggy black hair away from his forehead. Lines of suffering drew his mouth taut, and he gazed at nothing out of listless brown eyes. The other stranger stalked about like a lion on the prowl, hands jammed deep in the pockets of his black jacket and his face flushed with anger. His strongly-made features had a grim set that went well with his flinty eyes. Regina knelt beside the couch, her face white and drawn with worry. Lee was nowhere to be seen.

"What you say may be true, but this is not the time or place to explode," Sean warned the pacing man. He gestured to the man lying on the couch. "Rod won't make it if you can't stay cool. Calm down and think."

"Calm!" The man towered over Sean, his eyes snapping with fury. "We've been betrayed, the whole network endangered, and you want me to be a block of ice! 'Stay cool, Alec. Watch your temper, Alec.' I've been holding it back for years! I've had to smile and pretend while my mouth turns bitter with hate. Don't play psychologist with me, Sean! Don't preach mediocrity to me!"

"Sit down, and I'll preach you a new sermon." Sean's voice was inflexible as steel. The two men's eyes locked in a battle of wills. The room was dead silent. Finally Alec growled something unintelligible and threw himself into an armchair. Sean Krueger continued in a gentler tone of voice.

"You seem to think you're the only one playing at double agent. We work just as hard as you do for these people, and we get just as angry as you do. You think it's easy for us to hide what we feel? Too often we have to push back despair or hate. If we don't, it eats away at our hearts. We made a promise to protect Rod's people. When you made that promise you took on all the risks and dangers that come with it. Play-acting and deception are part of it. So is the possibility of betrayal. If you can't handle it, you'd better get out before you become the traitor."

Alec rubbed his forehead and stared guiltily at Mr. Krueger. "I get it, I get it. I just trumpeted your position to the neighbors."

"They'll draw their own conclusions."

"Marital discord?"

"Usually."

"I'm sorry, Sean."

"You're forgiven. Just don't let the anger consume you."

"Thanks, parson," Alec said wryly.

Lee materialized from a corner with an armload of clothes, and the argument was forgotten. Rod gathered enough energy to shuffle to the bathroom for a quick change. The Krueger family dispersed to gather food, flashlights, anything they could think of for the two men. Rod took his pack with a grateful nod while Alec relayed details about the raid.

"They knew we were coming," he said as he pushed his arm through the strap of a rucksack. "They ambushed us from behind the Keenes' house."

Sean frowned. "And the Keenes?"

"About half of the GSD squad went in the house, half chased us down the street. Give it a couple hours, and I bet you'll hear of their arrest on the early news. Poor souls."

Regina sat down in a wing chair, white-faced and trembling. "What can we do?"

"Nothing," her husband admitted as he came to rub her shoulder. "We let our inside man do his job. And we don't worry. They can't reveal any part of the organization the GSD doesn't already know about. But what about you, Alec?"

The big man said grimly, "I'll be moving on to another city, staying underground for a while."

"I'll miss you, my friend."

"I'll see you on the other side. Afraid you'll have to find someone else to preach to."

Laugh lines gathered around Sean Krueger's eyes as he shook Alec's hand.

Nausea rolled and bubbled in Allison's stomach. She retreated carefully down the hall and crept back into her bed, shaky from the pain that lanced her feet. She burrowed like a mole under the covers and stared at the spinning ceiling. It wasn't long before Lee slipped into the room and the house grew quiet again. Allison was too foggy to think about what she'd overheard. She just wanted to sleep for days and days.

*         *         *

As it turned out, Allison felt much more alert the next morning. She wandered cautiously about the house on aching feet. It was relatively small, rambling, and only one story high. There were three bedrooms, one with an antique pine bed for guests, all clustered on one side of the house. The hallway opened from there to the entryway and a spacious family room filled with creamy white furniture. The walls were decorated with oil paintings of nature scenes and portraits of the Kruegers. Allison could stand for hours just marveling at the deft strokes of color that looked like leaves, but she was much more intrigued by the lifelike studies of people – particularly a lovely portrait of Lee.

An arched doorway led from the family room to a honey-colored kitchen dominated by a heavy oak table and sturdy chairs. Pieces of white and blue china brightened the nooks and counters, and a pair of French doors opened to an inviting stone patio. Allison explored the pantry and the refrigerator, tempted by the delicious array of foods.

But it was the light-filled library Allison immediately fell in love with. In the quiet hours of the early afternoon, when Lee was in school and her parents at work, Allison brought a snack to one of the cushioned window seats in the library and curled up in the warm sun. Bookcases lined the walls from floor to ceiling. Two worn leather armchairs and a slim-legged table sat companionably at one of the room, and a set of French doors at the other end led to the patio.

And the books—history, philosophy, language, religion, mysteries, economics, art, poetry—sent a siren call to her hungry mind. But she didn't allow herself to touch them. Regina found her staring at the shelves, drew out a thin book, and placed it gently in Allison's hands. Allison turned each page reverently and lightly traced the neat rows of letters.

"Can you read?" Regina asked kindly.

"A little. We had to learn basic things for jobs."

"Just the basics?"

"Yeah. The orphanage sent me out to fix things. I know lots about electrical wiring and computers."

"Oh... I see. Well, you read any book you want. There's a dictionary on the round table by the sofa if you get stuck, and I'll be in the kitchen."

Allison frowned at the long word D-word.

"It tells you what words mean," Regina explained quickly. "It lists them by their order in the alphabet. And if that doesn't make sense, come ask me."

Allison's gaze was fastened on the pages, so she didn't see the ache in Regina's eyes as she turned away. Allison plopped down in an overstuffed easy chair and cradled the precious volume in her lap, intent on absorbing every word of it. Every now and then she tried to consult the unwieldy dictionary, but it didn't help at all; it used even more confusing words to explain the ones she couldn't understand. She had to admit she was stumped.

Lee entered the room to find her guest gazing absentmindedly out the window, one finger marking her page.

"You're not supposed to be sad on such a beautiful afternoon," Lee teased her. "Keep frowning like that, and we'll think you want to go back to the orphanage."

Allison smiled weakly.

"What are you reading?" Lee asked as she dropped to the floor at Allison's feet.

"I don't know. I never read anything like it. The words are in some kind of pattern, and it's confusing."

"Let's see where you are.... Allison, this is poetry."

"Okay." It was more of a question.

"It's an art form, like painting. The writer uses the best words he can think of to draw pictures in your head or create emotions. Or just to give you an idea. Listen to these lines....

> To see a World in a Grain of Sand
> And a Heaven in a Wild Flower,
> Hold Infinity in the palm of your hand
> And Eternity in an hour."

"It sounds good. What does it mean?"

"Since I'm not William Blake, I can't fully explain it. To me it means we must... um.... Come outside a minute."

Lee jumped up, grabbed Allison's hand, and pulled her through the French doors. The patio was still cool from the night's condensation. Allison stepped gingerly to the edge of it, but Lee took several steps across the sparkling grass. She stopped in a patch of sunlight that burnished her hair to a rich gold.

"Come on," she coaxed.

Allison shifted on the icy stones and glanced anxiously at the neighbor's house over the tall, weathered fence. Were those people home? And walking around barefoot outside was strange enough, but on wet grass? She peered anxiously at the lawn.

"I'm not supposed to be outside. Somebody might see me."

"The Christensens are on vacation as of yesterday, and nobody can see through the maple trees near the back."

"Are you sure?"

"I promise. Come into the sun!" Lee spread her arms and cocked her head, eyes shining with mirth.

Mentally scolding herself for being afraid, Allison stepped tentatively into the grass. Its pliable softness surprised her, and she instantly loved the feathery sensation. She padded forward until she stood in the sun with Lee. It was so quiet she could hear an animal skittering around in a nearby tree. There were no neighbors peeking over fences, no dogs barking feverishly, nothing but branches rustling in the wind.

"Time is different out here," Lee said at last, a faraway look about her face. "When we slow down, get off our racetrack lives, we can put time in its place. We've forgotten that life is more than a ticking clock, and we've become slaves to our schedules. The world is such a beautiful place, and it's always changing. To truly appreciate it, to really enjoy it, we must master time."

"That's what the poetry means?"

"The poem. Yes, that's what I get out of it."

"Then why didn't he just write that?"

"It's the way he wrote it that catches our attention. The human brain loves a puzzle. Didn't it tease your brain?"

"Yeah." Allison's face cleared as the meaning sank in. "But I couldn't do that at the orphanage, slow down I mean. I understand that part. Why do you want to enjoy the world?"

"For me it's a big part of being truly alive."

Regina poked her head out the door. "Lee, come inside!"

The girls sauntered back through the soft grass and quick-stepped across the cold patio into the kitchen. Regina pulled the door closed behind them, craning her head to survey of the yard. She folded her arms and faced Lee with an uncharacteristic frown. Allison sidled to the kitchen table and sat down. *Oh, she's mad!* Her eyes darted between mother and daughter as if she could see the tension boiling between them.

"Lee, Allison is supposed to stay inside. It's not safe for her to be out there yet, and you know it."

"Mom, it's just the back yard. No one was watching. The nosy people are on vacation, remember?"

Allison's eyes widened at Lee's breezy tone. Regina's expression remained the same, and her voice was calm and even.

"Yes, I know. None of that excuses the fact that you ignored the rules and placed our guest in danger."

Lee shrugged, bewildered. "Well, I'm sorry. I won't do it again."

"This is not a game, Lee," Regina's voice rose a little. "She is not one of your school friends staying the weekend. You're playing with her life! With our lives!"

Lee blinked.

"You may not use the car today," Regina continued, in control once more. "While you're walking to the meeting, I want you to think about the situation here. Take your snack with you. You'll be late."

Regina turned and went swiftly to the counter where a batter-caked mixing bowl waited for her. Allison looked away from her friend's shocked face, embarrassed to have been the cause of such a scene. Her gaze snagged on a red armband with a bold, crooked X stamped on a white circle. The blood in her face drained, and her muscles locked together. *No, not here!*

Lee moved into her peripheral vision and picked up the armband. Allison watched the hideous thing wrap around her friend's arm, right over her shirt sleeve. Her eyes shot up to Lee's face. The girl frowned slightly, still bewildered. She left the kitchen without speaking to either Allison or her mother and closed the front door softly behind her.

"Regina."

The lady whirled around. "What's wrong, honey?" Seeing Allison's white face, she swiftly wiped her hands and rounded the table to kneel at Allison's side. "What is it?"

"That thing Lee put on. Why is it here? What is she doing with it?"

Relief smoothed the worry lines from Regina's face. She held Allison's hand in both of her own. "Honey, Lee is part of the Hitler Youth Club. It's mandatory for our children to join; she doesn't have a choice. Don't think she.... Don't think we believe any bit of their lies. We have nothing to do with the people who kept you in that orphanage."

Allison drew a shaky breath and slouched in her chair.

"It's a good cover, isn't it?" Regina asked with a bitter smile.

"Yeah," Allison agreed. "A good cover."

# 11

**Y**ou could have told me how much soap to use."

"Ha! You should have seen your eyes! I swear they were this big!" Lee made her long fingers touch in a circle and held it up.

Allison scrunched her eyes at the blatant exaggeration.

"It really was funny," Lee said plaintively. She lowered her hands slowly.

Allison thought back to the mountains of bubbles surging out of the bathtub. She'd been mortified, just standing with the empty soap bottle dangling from one hand and watching the bubbles grow exponentially. If Lee hadn't knocked on the door then, they might have taken over the entire bathroom.

"I guess it was pretty funny," she admitted with a self-conscious laugh.

Lee chuckled and wrapped her in a hug. "Don't worry. You're learning quickly, but you can't expect to get everything right on the first try."

"Sounds like something your dad would say."

"Actually," Lee said sheepishly, "I *was* quoting him."

Allison pulled away and looked up at her friend. "But you always seem so happy and confident. You don't make that many mistakes, do you?"

"Confident. Yes. That's probably why I do; I'm so sure I'm right all the time, and I don't always think about what I'm doing.

That's what Dad tells me. I think I proved him right this afternoon." Remorse filled her voice. "I'm very sorry about that."

"It's okay. I broke the rules, too."

They were silent for a minute.

"What happens to you?" Allison wanted to know. "When you make mistakes."

Lee frowned. "Depends on what I've done. Nothing more than a lecture usually. Did they punish you for mistakes at the orphanage?"

*The Asian boy wrapped an arm around his head as the security guard drew back a black-booted foot to kick him again.* Allison winced at the memory. "Yes. For mistakes and accidents. Sometimes for nothing at all."

A gentle knock sounded on the bedroom door.

"May I come in?" came Sean's voice.

"Sure, Dad," Lee answered as she reached over to open the door for him.

Sean took a step forward and leaned against the doorframe. His face softened and crinkled as his daughter came to hug him. Resting his chin on her sleek head, he remarked, "I see you've been beautifying yourselves. How did you like your bath, Allison?"

"Not so much," Allison replied, smoothing her wet hair.

Sean's eyebrows shot up. "Really?"

"I mean, I'm not sure it liked me."

Lee smothered a giggle in her dad's suit jacket.

"Well, I can see there's a story to be told," Sean said, "but you'll have to tell me later. Allison, there's an important man from our resistance group here to see you. Are you up to answering a few questions?"

Allison knotted her fingers nervously.

"He just wants to know about the orphanage," Sean said gently.

She relaxed a little. "I think I'm up to it."

"Okay." He wrapped a fatherly arm around her shoulders.

"Would you wait here, Lee?"

Lee nodded, the twinkle in her eyes subsiding at the grave tone of her father's question. "You want to talk about this afternoon."

"Yes. I'll be right back."

Sean led Allison to the family room. Two table lamps cast a dim glow from either ends of the white couch, gently illuminating the man sitting in the middle of it. The man rose stiffly as they entered the room, and Allison was surprised to see that he was very old and almost as little as she.

"Allison, this gentleman is one of the founders of our organization. We call him 'Papa.'"

Papa hobbled forward with a gnarled hand extended, and a lovely smile split his withered-apple face.

"So nice to meet you." His voice was wispy but genuine.

"And you, sir," she responded as held his quivering hand very gently.

"Very good, very good," he said, nodding his silver head and beaming at her. He released her hand, turned slowly back to the couch, and eased himself down with a sigh.

"Sean, would you give us an hour alone? Thank you."

Sean acquiesced with a nod and went back down the hall.

"Now, young lady," Papa said kindly, "why don't you have a seat next to me?"

Allison's tension was eased by the old man's manner and appearance, and she went to sit carefully by the resistance patriarch. In his worn gray sweater and khaki slacks, he looked perfectly harmless, unobtrusive, and grandfatherly. *What kind of job does he do for them?* she wondered as she met his mild brown eyes. She decided the position he held must be an honorary one, for such a fragile man would never be able to spy on the GSD or ferry escapees from one safe house to another.

"This is an unexpected pleasure," he quavered. "You are the first to successfully escape from an orphanage, a marvelous breakthrough for our organization. We have been helping oppressed men and women escape from labor camps for years, but we have not been able to find even a crack in orphanage security. I beg your pardon...."

Papa rummaged through his pants pocket and produced a slim, black object.

"May I record our conversation? It's for my colleagues' benefit."

"Sure."

The old man placed the small recorder on the cushion between them, pressed a button, and cleared his throat noisily. "August 23. Roughly nine-thirty in the evening. Interview with escaped child named Allison." He paused and fastened his mild eyes on her. "Now, my dear, I have interviewed the boy you know as Zip and gathered details of your bold escape. He also told me that you know something that may endanger your life, something to do with an extermination plan. We would like to know exactly what you know about it, how you found out, and who the information came from."

"I don't know where to start," she floundered.

Papa smiled benevolently, folding his gnarled fingers in his lap. "Why don't you start with the conversation you overheard, and we'll go on from there."

She gave her account of the conversation between the decontamination director and the nurse, the meeting with Cuba and Zip, and how the three of them pieced the information together.

"Were any dates or timelines mentioned?" Papa asked.

"Nothing specific. Just that it's a few months away."

"They're ahead of schedule then. Any idea how it's to be done? Where the children are being taken?"

"No."

"Hum." Papa gazed at the wall opposite where a painting of a willow tree trailing its branches in a river hung. A comfortable silence settled between them as the old man pondered the information. Allison pulled her knees up to her chest, rested her cheek on them, and watched him gather his thoughts.

"Well, we will work those out later," Papa said at last. "Now, tell me all about your daily routine at the orphanage. Every detail, even if it seems trivial to you."

Allison took a deep breath and told him all she could remember. Bland meals, jobs in the city, security guards always watching, black walls sliding down to encase her in a tomb of silence—it all flowed out of her into Papa's little recording device. Only once he stopped her to reset it. She talked until her memory dried up and she caught herself stifling yawns mid-sentence.

"I am tiring you with all my questions," Papa said when he caught those yawns. "That should be enough for tonight. You and I need our rest."

"Papa?" Allison asked hesitantly.

His kindly eyes turned back to her.

"Papa, why do you think they're still hunting for me? Why can't they let me go?"

"Ah. Let's apply a little logic to that. If you had told the other children what you overheard, what would they have done?"

Allison rubbed her cheek against the soft fleece of her pajama pants. "I think they would've been scared."

"They might have panicked?"

"Yes."

"They might have refused to go to work or tried to escape. Those larger boys might have overpowered the guards and staged a rebellion. It would have been quite a problem. Yes. I wonder they didn't isolate you immediately."

"The decon director and the nurse could've lost their jobs for talking policy in front of me."

Papa nodded repeatedly. "They would indeed. Better to keep the incident to themselves, they thought. Good reasoning, my dear, very good reasoning."

"But I escaped with Zip...." Allison said slowly.

"And brought that invaluable nugget of information to us," Papa finished for her.

"Ohhhhh." Allison groaned and pressed her forehead against her knees. Papa patted her shoulder clumsily.

"Yes, yes. They must find you to punish you and to uncover

our resistance group. But we will move faster. We will use your information to construct a rescue operation."

"Rescue?" Allison raised her head.

"To be sure," Papa nodded encouragingly. "Thanks to you, we can now look for the weak points in the orphanage system and finally penetrate it. We'll pass the information on to our subgroups in other cities so they can synchronize with us. Think of it – in one night, all the orphans in the country could be freed!"

Hope surged in Allison's heart, and she smiled hugely. Papa chuckled and patted her forearm. "I know how anxious you are for your friends. Well, you will see them soon–free, as you are."

He picked up the recorder and pressed the button before stowing it in his pants pocket. Holding the edge of the couch with both hands, he leaned forward to rise. Allison put her feet down and held Papa's bony arm to brace him as they stood together. He bent slightly to pick up a brown shapeless hat from the coffee table and placed it carefully on his head.

"Ahhh. Thank you. Thank you." He turned haltingly to face her. "You had better stay in the house a bit longer."

"Okay." She had hoped to go out with Lee, but....

"We will meet again, I think, for another interview. Before I go, what can you tell me about your parents?"

Fragments of dreams and hazy memories flitted through her mind. "Not much," she admitted sadly.

"And what was your ID number?"

"A160434."

"Good, good. We will see what we can do about finding your folks."

Her heart pounded with elation. "You can do that?"

"Thanks to certain acquired computer chips, we can try." A roguish twinkle in his eyes, Papa offered his ancient hand. Allison shook it gratefully, grinning with pure delight.

"Good-bye, my dear."

"Good-bye, Papa."

The old man turned and shuffled into the kitchen, and

Allison heard the patio door click softly behind him.

*          *          *

Two hollow knocks sounded on the wood door.

"Enter!" the Director called crisply.

A bulky man with heavy-lidded eyes stepped through the door, one thin manila folder clutched in his powerful hands. The Director cast a few papers to one side, folding his hands and gazing expectantly at his visitor.

"You must do something about your appearance, Gunther," he chided, eyeing the strained fabric of the other man's cheap suit. "You do not blend in here."

Gunther shrugged his shoulders belligerently. "I fit in fine on the streets. Which is what you pay me for."

He tossed the folder on the Director's desk and crossed his arms, stretching the seams of his jacket across his muscular shoulders. His boss grunted as he flipped the file open to read the one-page report. Gunther watched motionlessly. When he finished his perusal, the Director leaned back in his leather chair and smoothed his fingers over the glossy armrests.

"I commend you, Gunther, on your efficiency and your brevity. It is unfortunate that the Keenes left us so soon, and without obliging my curious nature. However, our operative seems to be in a good position to provide us with other subjects. What is your evaluation?"

"It looks good. He was accepted without rigorous questioning and is now working in their safe house system. But we should wait several weeks before we attempt to capture any more of the traitors."

"Agreed." The Director rose abruptly and rounded the desk to stand in front of Gunther. "Tell our man we want younger subjects, deeply embedded in the system, who can divulge more weighty secrets." He perched on the edge of his desk, eyes glazed over with thought. "I want the identity of Papa."

"Sir," Gunther protested gruffly, "we have not penetrated that deeply! Our operative can only give us the smaller members of the group. We must wait until–"

"Did I ask for your opinion?" the Director interrupted in a deceptively mild voice.

Gunther shut his mouth with a click.

The Director stepped in close and locked eyes with his underling. He spoke slowly and deliberately. "I want Papa. We cannot destroy the body of the resistance without first removing the brain. Tell the operative to burrow deep. Find someone who knows Papa personally. We will break contact so he may focus exclusively and without interruption on this one task. That is all."

Gunther nodded curtly and turned away.

"Gunther."

The big man halted mid-step.

"Any news about the missing orphans?"

Gunther swiveled his head to speak over his shoulder. "Not yet. I will find them soon."

"That is good," the Director said smoothly. "I really do hate failure."

Gunther strode hastily from the room.

# 12

Allison sat in Sean's leather desk chair, her back to the open window. A warm breeze scented with roses and freshly-cut grass teased her hair, but all her attention was focused on the smooth baritone voice coming from the radio on the bookshelf. She stared at the knobs and yellowed station numbers on the ancient set while her fingers twisted a bit of copper wire in her lap.

"Thank you for joining us today. This is Kurt Jensen bringing you the elevated thoughts and fiery words of our first Leader, Adolf Hitler. We read to become more like him. We read that the past may not be forgotten and the future ensured. An excerpt from *My Struggle,* chapter 5, Philosophies and Organization, page 423...."

Allison rounded the desk and peeked into the living room. Sean was seated on the couch, head bent over his dog-eared Bible, his fingers lightly turning the translucent pages. Next to him Regina perched with one leg curled beneath her. She hummed and softly plucked at the strings of a shabby guitar. Lee curled up in the big easy chair and combed her fingers through her hair while she tossed out song titles for her parents' approval.

Today was Sunday, and this was the Krueger family's church service.

Easing the door shut, Allison went back to her seat at the desk. She leaned forward to turn up the volume on the radio. Cover the worship music, that was her job.

"Why can't you just sing as loud as you want?" she'd asked Regina while the two washed the breakfast dishes.

"It's illegal to be a Christian," Regina said as she scoured a greasy pan. "If our neighbors heard us, they'd report us to the police. We'd end up in jail with life sentences at the least."

"But I've seen churches in the city."

"No." Regina's hands stilled in the soapy water. She shook an escaped tendril of hair out of her face and looked sorrowfully at Allison. "They may call those buildings churches, but they do not worship God there. They worship Adolf Hitler."

Confused, Allison picked at a chip in the blue ceramic bowl she was drying. *God. What is God?*

The melodic voice on the radio interrupted her thoughts.

"...but imperiously demands, not only its own exclusive and unlimited recognition, but the complete transformation of all public life in accordance with its views. It can, therefore, not tolerate the simultaneously continuance of a body representing the former condition. - This is equally true of religions...."

Allison looked up from the wire she'd twisted into a corkscrew.

"...Christianity could not content itself with building up its own altar; it was absolutely forced to undertake the destruction of the heathen altars. Only from this fanatical intolerance could its apodictic faith take form; this intolerance is, in fact, its absolute presupposition...."

*Fanatical intolerance.* She mouthed the words to herself and resolved to look them up later.

"...The objection may very well be raised that such phenomena in world history arise for the most part from specifically Jewish modes of thought, in fact, that this type of intolerance and fanaticism positively embodies the Jewish nature...."

She raised her head as a particularly lovely strain of music superimposed itself over the radio program.

Behold Him there the risen Lamb,
My perfect spotless righteousness,
The great unchangeable I AM,
The King of glory and of grace,
One in Himself I cannot die.
My soul is purchased by His blood,
My life is hid with Christ on high,
With Christ my Savior and my God!


Allison nudged the volume up to cover the rising song.

"...The individual may establish with pain today that with the appearance of Christianity the first spiritual terror entered into the far freer ancient world, but he will not be able to contest the fact that since then the world has been afflicted and dominated by this coercion, and that coercion is broken only by coercion, and terror only by terror....."

*Terror. Afflicted. Coercion.* The words were strange, but they seethed with the same tone the orphanage guards used when they talked about the kids: hateful.

Allison got up and laid her ear against the door.


Take my will, and make it Thine;
It shall be no longer mine:
Take my heart, it is Thine own;
It shall be Thy royal throne,
It shall be Thy royal throne.

Take my love, my Lord, I pour
At Thy feet its treasure store:
Take myself, and I will be
Ever, only, all for Thee,
Ever, only, all for Thee.


She drew back and stared at the wood grain without seeing it. Strange, beautiful words. Love songs to a mysterious person. She returned to her chair and swiveled to face the window. Drawing her knees up to her chin, she watched the gauzy curtains sway and lift with the wind.

*             *             *

"You're up awfully early."

Allison jumped a little and dropped the wooden spoon she was using to stir her scrambled eggs. Sean smiled tiredly as he adjusted a navy blue tie around the collar of his crisply pressed shirt.

"It's 5:35," he said with a glance at the benighted glass of the patio doors.

"Oh! Yes. I couldn't sleep." Allison gingerly tapped the spoon away from the hot burner and picked it up. "Would you like some eggs?"

"Mmmm." Sean circled the big table to lean over the range. "I think so. You know, they cook well if you stir them continuously and keep the heat a bit lower. There you go."

He adjusted the knob for her and stepped aside to the burbling coffee pot. Allison stirred the yellow lumps carefully and watched for the wet sheen to disappear. Then she moved the skillet to a cool burner and scooped half of her concoction onto a blue-edged plate for Sean. He finished stirring the cream into his coffee and speared a bit of egg. Allison watched apprehensively as he chewed.

"That's pretty good. All it needs is salt and pepper."

"Oh." Allison's face fell. "I forgot."

"It's easily remedied. The salt and pepper shakers are next to that brown jar, there on your left. Why don't you bring your plate to the table."

Sean picked up his plate and mug and moved toward the table, but he lurched and sloshed some of the hot liquid on the floor.

"Coffee!"

Allison started. Was that an order?

"Cat," Sean grumbled good-naturedly. "Sorry, Allison. I tripped over Coffee."

"Oh." Allison reached for the yellow hand towel that hung on the oven handle. "Would you like me to get you some more?"

"No, thank you." He took the proffered towel and bent to wipe up the spill. "Yes, yes. I know you're hungry. Let's eat, Your Highness."

Coffee jogged after Sean to the pantry, meowing insistently. Allison searched through the fruit basket for an apple before she took her plate to the table. Sean joined her a minute later.

"So," he said between bites, "why couldn't you sleep this morning?"

"We used to get up around six at the orphanage," she hedged. "Guess I can't break the habit."

"No." He rejected her statement gently. "Something's worrying you."

Allison lowered her gaze to her fork, scraped the tines soundlessly across her plate.

"You don't have to confide in me. Though I am willing to listen to anything you'd like to share."

She glanced at Sean from the corner of her eyes. He rested his elbows on the table and watched her with that tender look in his eyes, the one he always had for Lee. She put her fork down deliberately.

"I'm what's worrying me."

Sean waited in companionable silence for her to continue. Allison focused on his folded hands.

"I'm inferior. I looked it up in the dictionary, but I still don't understand. It doesn't tell me why. We must have done something wrong. Do you know what it is? I just don't...."

Sean reached over and raised her chin. "They had no right to label you or your ancestors with that word." His fingers shook, and his eyes bored into hers with a steely intensity.

"You're angry," Allison said in shock.

"I am furious," Sean corrected her in a tight voice. "It is the Germans' one-word excuse for theft, slavery, and ultimately murder."

"You mean...."

"Yes. That is the bare, shameful truth of it. There is nothing inferior about your people; it was only for their own gain, an excuse for war and domination, that they call you that." He squeezed Allison's hand fiercely. "It is a lie. Don't you believe it!"

Her heart warmed, melting the old pain into tears that escaped unchecked to rain on her shirt.

"Come here, honey." Sean stood and opened his arms. She went without hesitation and cuddled her head against his bony chest. His thin arms held her shoulders tightly, just as Allison had seen him hug his own daughter so many times. She tipped her head back. Sean gazed sorrowfully down at her.

"I am so sorry," he said in a low voice, "for all the abuse you have endured. I wish I could erase it."

"Thank you," Allison replied softly. "It wasn't you, though."

Sean sighed and released her. "Yes. Well. That's a conversation for another day. I have to go to work." He glanced at his watch, then back at her. "Thank you for breakfast. And for sharing with me."

Allison nodded.

Sean lifted his suit jacket from the back of his chair and thrust his arms into it. Allison watched him tug it into place, her mind sifting their conversation to find an incongruous word.

"Sean?"

"Hm?"

"Who are the Germans?"

He blinked confusedly. "Did I say that?"

"Yes."

He smoothed his lapel thoughtfully. "The short answer is half of the people in this country, from the Director of the GSD to the newspaper man on the street. At least half are Germans."

Allison sorted through this. "But you are not."

"No." Sean shook his head. "My people were here before the Germans came."

"Zip said some people took over this country. He said they're trying to eat the whole world. Are they the Germans?"

"Yes. Yes, they are."

"How did they..." She stopped as a ton of questions dumped themselves into her mind. "Why... What happened here?"

Sean smoothed her hair softly. "That story is best told by someone else."

Allison nodded and left it alone. Sean patted her shoulder and walked quickly to the front door. He disappeared into the dusky summer morning, and the door eased shut behind him. Allison looked indecisively at the small mound of dishes she'd created. She yawned widely. It could wait.

*Terror. Fear.*

Allison rubbed at her puffy eyes as she headed for the bedroom. She knew those feelings well, and there had been none of that in her heart when she had revealed her thoughts to Sean. He had been so gentle with her, but so fiercely angry with the Germans. Allison untied her robe slowly. So angry, and that had almost frightened her. *But*, she realized, *he was angry because I have been hurt. He was angry for me.*

She wrapped herself tightly in her blankets and let her swollen eyelids close.

\*                    \*                    \*

The afternoon sun rested lazily on Allison's face, and she brought her fingers to her mouth to cover a wide yawn. She snuggled deeper into the couch and gently turned the page of her book about American history. Its spine was threadbare and faded, and the pages were growing yellow with age, but the pictures were still vibrant. Men in odd, formal suits; strange machines and vehicles; clans of wild, painted men riding to war; black and white photographs of perfectly flat fields and pine-topped mountains..... Lee had complained when her father added this tome to her homework load, insisting she know something more about the land she lived in. Curious, Allison had borrowed the book to while away the morning, but the stories had captured her imagination for the past six hours. At some point Regina had joined her with a tray of thin crackers, sliced muenster cheese, and two glasses of ice water. The older lady quietly perused her own book, and the two enjoyed their companionable silence.

Four heavy-handed knocks reverberated through the living room.

Allison's head snapped up to meet Regina's wide blue eyes.

"A friend?" she asked tenuously.

"No, I'm not expecting anyone."

Four more knocks sounded on the front door.

Regina sat ramrod straight in her arm chair and lowered her book by degrees to the coffee table. "Allison." Her voice was tranquil and low. "Go to the hall. Stay out of sight. If they come in, go to my bedroom."

Allison almost fell out of her chair in her hurry to obey. She flattened herself against the wall and peeked around the edge. Regina rose and walked deliberately to the door. She stood there for a minute, drew in a deep breath before opening it.

"Yes?"

"Good afternoon, ma'am," came a smooth deep voice. "We're sorry to disturb you, but have you seen this man?"

Regina took a paper the unseen man gave her and scanned it. "No, I can't help you."

She returned it with a polite smile and moved to shut the door. A large, blunt-fingered hand shot out to hold it back.

"I'm sorry, ma'am, but we have a few more questions. May we come in?"

He was already stepping through the door, a tall powerfully built man wearing a gray suit that strained at the seams. Regina was forced to step back to allow him and his companion, a slightly shorter man neatly attired in tan, to enter the foyer. The trim man smiled genially as he shut the door and leaned against it with folded arms. Regina's eyes flicked to Allison.

"He was last seen in this neighborhood," the first man said.

Allison inched backward several feet, then turned and ran on soft feet to the master bedroom. With trembling fingers she lifted the white bed skirt of the old four-poster and squirmed underneath. She flattened herself to the floor and lay still.

A latch clicked.

Allison breathed through her nose. *Too loud!*

The bed skirt lifted, and Lee's inquisitive face appeared.

Allison let out a harsh breath in relief.

"What are you doing in here, Allison?"

"Hiding."

"This is the worst place—"

"Didn't you hear those two men come in?"

"No, I didn't. Scoot over."

Lee crawled in next to her and lay on her belly with her chin pillowed on her hands.

"What do they want?" she whispered.

"A man, they said. They're looking for a man." Allison lowered her forehead to the carpet and swallowed drily.

"Hey." Lee rubbed her shoulder. "It's okay. They're not looking for you."

"What if they search the house?"

Lee didn't respond. Her fingers tightened on Allison's shoulder and remained there. The rumbling voices of the men alternated with Regina's quietly courteous tones.

Back and forth, question and answer.

Allison squirmed against the ache in her stiff back. All the air seemed to be gone, and she breathed dust instead.

Masculine feet tramped into the hall, into one of the other bedrooms. Wood creaked against wood as dresser drawers opened and shut, and the distinctive voices of squeaky hinges and sticky latches rose in protest. The footsteps came closer.

"How many children do you have?"

"Two. Two girls."

"Whose rooms are these?"

"The guest room and my room."

"I'll distract them," Lee said abruptly. She crawled out and climbed to her feet, paused for a minute, and went swiftly around the bed to a tall bookcase. Paper whispered against wood as she drew a book from one of the shelves and opened it. The door swung open suddenly, and a pair of scuffed black shoes walked in.

Allison's blood froze.

"Who are you?" the man asked in clipped tones.

"Anneliese Krueger," Lee answered in kind. The book shut with a firm thump. "This is my house. Who are *you*?"

The man ignored her saucy manner. "What are you doing in here?"

"Looking for a book. And you? Did my mother let you in or did you break in?"

*Stop it, Lee!* Allison begged mentally. *Don't make him mad!*

"Anyone else in the house?"

"No."

"Where's your sister?"

"Not here."

He grunted. The black shoes went to the opposite end of the room and wrenched open the louvered closet doors. Clothing rustled and shoes thumped. The shoes backed away and paused, toes pointed at the bed.

A scream built in the back of Allison's throat, and she clamped a hand over her mouth.

"Gunther!" a man's voice called. "Where are you?"

"Here!" The shoes went rapidly to the door and met a pair of brown ones.

"Found it," the voice said triumphantly.

"Where?"

"House behind this one. Old lady across the street said she saw our man leaving the front yard with another fellow. Owners are on a month-long vacation. Perfect hide-out."

"Show me," Gunther demanded.

Both sets of shoes disappeared from sight, and the front door shut firmly a minute later. Allison's breath came out in one noisy gasp, and she realized she hadn't been breathing for the last minute. She dropped her whirling head into her hands. The bed skirt rustled as Lee picked up the edge of it.

"Are you okay?" Her voice was tense, almost harsh.

"No," Allison croaked into the carpet fibers.

"Come on out. You can't breathe under there."

Lee tugged gently but insistently at Allison's left arm until she came out. They sat down together on the multi-colored quilt, and Lee gently smoothed her staticky hair as she cried uncontrollably.

"It's okay now," Lee soothed her. "That's just the adrenaline working itself out of your system."

"No-o," Allison hiccupped. She swallowed and regained some control. "I can't... go back. You...don't understa-and! You don't understand!"

Allison sobbed harder, her lungs heaving in and out like a great bellows. She wrapped her arms around her ribs in a vain attempt to hold them in. The bed dipped a little on her right, and Regina's arms enfolded her in a soft, firm hug. Allison pressed her face against Regina's shoulder and didn't move for a long time.

# 13

The house was silent when Allison padded down the hall at the usual dinner time. She sniffled through her swollen nose and hugged her arms around the faded terrycloth robe. She stopped at the edge of the living room. One lamp glowed dimly from a side table, and the kitchen was entirely dark. A bar of light showed under the office door. Allison rubbed her nose, went over and knocked tentatively.

"Come on in," Sean called.

"Where are Lee and Regina?" she asked as she came to sit in the little high-backed chair by his desk.

Sean leaned back, and his chair creaked. He swiveled to face her, and she saw a thick leather-bound book lying open in his lap.

"They've gone out for the evening," he answered as he settled his forearms on the worn armrests. "They seemed pretty shaken up, so I thought they should have a little time away."

Allison looked down and picked at a stray thread on her cuff.

"If you're hungry, I can whip up some dinner for us," Sean offered.

"Maybe later."

"How are you doing?" he asked softly.

"Okay."

Sean was silent.

"No, not okay," Allison amended. "I was really frightened.

They almost found me. They would've found me and sent me back to die."

"But they didn't."

"No."

Sean's chair creaked as he shifted a little. "Lee was too scattered to tell me about it. What made them leave the house?"

"One of them said they'd found the hiding place of the men they were looking for, and they both left."

"Just as the first man began to search my room."

Something in his tone caught Allison's attention. She looked up straight into his twinkling brown eyes. A curious smile spread over his face, and he tapped the arms of the chair excitedly. "That is a true miracle!"

"A what?"

"A miracle. A wonderful, unexplainable thing God did."

Allison stared doubtfully at him. "Nothing wonderful happened. It was just the timing that saved me."

"Yes, exactly. That's just the way God like to do things."

"How do you know?"

Sean laid both hands on the book in his lamp. "This book is called the Bible. It's full of stories of all the things God has done and messages he's given us."

Allison looked at the book, then back at Sean's inquisitive face.

"Have you never heard of God, Allison?"

She thought for a minute. "The orphanage guards all wear the same belts. 'God with us' is on the buckle."

"Ah, but they don't mean the God of the Bible. They mean a god they can control, use, and manipulate however they like."

"That's what Regina said: that they don't worship the same God. So what is he?"

"He's hard to explain." Sean looked at the pages beneath his fingers. "He is a perfect being: powerful, wise, loving, righteous.... He is eternal; He has always existed and always will."

"Where is He?"

"We can't see Him because He doesn't have a body like ours, but we can see traces of Him in nature and in our lives. He made us and the world, and He's always moving and doing things among us."

"If you can't see Him, how can you know that?" She gestured at the Bible. "Or that a man didn't make up all those stories?"

"That's the hard part, believing in what you can't see. We call it faith. Sometimes God shows Himself to us like He did to the writers of these stories. Sometimes we see Him through what He does in our lives. And sometimes we can feel and hear Him."

Allison picked at the hem of her robe, unsure of what to say.

Sean's voice sliced into her thoughts. "We breathe air, right? But we can't see it. We know it's there because of its effects, like the wind in the trees. God is much the same way."

Allison lifted her head and locked gazes with Sean. His eyes searched hers intently, full of conviction and sadness.

"When He made us, He put into us a knowledge of His existence. I used to feel like I'd lost something important and had to look for it. It was God's way of calling me to Him."

"Why?"

"Why did He call me? I was trying to control my life and breaking His laws, both very wrong."

Allison chewed thoughtfully on her lip. "So God wants to control your life? And you have to follow His rules?"

"'Control' might be a bad term. Umm....This might be a stretch, but think of God as a good fuhrer and the world as His land. The first people broke his laws, and now everyone refuses to obey them. What should he do with us?"

Allison shifted her weight. "Punish everyone, I guess."

"He has the right to, yes, but He loves all of us as if we were His own children. He doesn't want to punish us, but things had to be made right between us. So He came in human form, was born like every other baby, grew up, ate, slept, and worked like the rest of us. He walked all over the country he was born in, teaching the people about Himself and healing their sicknesses.

His name was Jesus." Sean's eyes clouded over with tears.

"He sounds nice," Allison blurted as she got to her feet. "I think I'll go get something to eat now. Can I get you anything?"

"No, but thank you." His tone was still gentle in spite of her abrupt ending of their conversation.

Allison nodded awkwardly and headed for the door.

"Allison?"

She turned back, playing nervously with her fingers.

"If you ever want to know more about Him, I'd be happy to talk with you."

She nodded again. "Okay."

Sean echoed her nod with an encouraging one of his own. She went to the kitchen with her mind turning uneasily. She had sat quietly as she tried to absorb and reconcile all this. But nothing connected or even coincided with anything she'd experienced in her life or seen of the world around her. The strange reasoning and fantastic stories sounded like something from a child's imaginative play. But she didn't want to hurt Sean with a statement like that.

Allison opened the refrigerator door and scanned the shelves with unseeing eyes.

An invisible person who made everything. Who might be anywhere, watching her, trying to control her. She wasn't sure she liked the idea.

# 14

Summer was at its high point. The sky was hazy with humidity, and the grass tips turned brown with their thirst for water. The Kruegers' neighbors emerged from their stifling houses to lounge on their porches and consume iced drinks while their kids walked around with dripping ice cream cones. Allison stretched and shifted restlessly on the library window seat. She sighed in frustration. *No news. No change. What if they've taken all the other orphans away?*

The front door closed. She watched Sean Krueger stroll down the walk to the mailbox. He waved to the older couple sitting on their porch swing across the street before he leaned around the metal container and opened it. Straightening again, he riffled the white envelopes. His fingers stopped abruptly. Head still bent over the letter, he came quickly back to the house.

"Allison!" The door shut on his excited call for her. "Allison!"

She slipped off her perch and trotted to the library door. Opening it, she stepped out and nearly crashed into Sean. He held two long envelopes out to her, both already torn open. A boyish smile crinkled every laugh line in his face, and his brown eyes shone with delight.

"Two for you," he announced. "One from Papa, and one from a friend."

Puzzled, she took the offered missives in both hands and looked at the handwriting. Papa's letter was addressed in precise block letters, and the other was an unfamiliar slanted scrawl.

*Who else would write me? Zip?*

Allison slid one finger under the flap and ripped it open. Her face cleared, and a smile teased the corners of her mouth. It *was* a letter from Zip.

*Dear Allison,*

*How do you like life on the outside? You haven't seen much of anything yet, but it's upside down from orphanage life. Right side up, I mean. I'm getting bored shut up in a house all day. I've started fixing things for my hosts. Radios, refrigerator, etc. Nice people, but I think they're trying to absorb me into their family. What do you think of the Kruegers? Nice people, too, but I can't stand all the God stuff.*

*Papa's been over a few times. He's working out all the details of the plan to rescue your buddies. He's the only company I have. I wish you could visit or at least talk on the telephone. You always seem impressed with my fountain of knowledge and my refined sense of humor. Everyone else pats me on the head or rolls their eyes. Okay, that's not strictly true. They do treat me like a child sometimes.*

*I'll see you soon, but write back anyway; I want to know what you've been up to.*

*Zip*

Allison let out a little guffaw of laughter and folded the letter.

"So how is he?"

She raised her head to meet Sean's expectant gaze. She'd forgotten he was still there. Sean raised his eyebrows.

"He's fine," Allison answered with a full-blown grin. "Bored, whiny, not very patient."

"That's him all right. Now have a look at what Papa sent."

Allison drew out a small piece of notepaper with no greeting or signature, just:

Let the little one out to play.

Her eyes shot up to meet Sean's. "Really?" she squeaked.

108

"If Papa says so, it's so," Sean replied, laughing.

Allison threw her arms around him in brief, tight hug and ran to the bedroom shouting for Lee. She crashed through the door, babbling and waving the note excitedly in her friend's face. Lee, who was sitting at her desk poring over her science homework, leaned back and chuckled.

"Slow down, girl, I can't understand you!"

"Sorry." Allison gulped some air. "He says—I can go out!"

Lee whooped and spun from her seat. "Finally! Come to the bathroom." She snagged Allison's wrist on her way out the door. "We can go out today if we do it right now."

"Do what? What're we doing?" Allison stumbled into the bathroom behind Lee.

The taller girl opened the mirror cabinet over the sink and produced a dark brown bottle with a flourish.

"Your disguise!" she announced gleefully, shaking the bottle. "I've been waiting so long for this! I bought this stuff for you *ages* ago. Well, days technically."

"Sorry, what're we doing?" Allison begged.

"Dyeing your hair," Lee shot over her shoulder as she rummaged through the shelves for towels. "Your dark hair and skin would attract attention, so we'll dye your hair a lighter color. Nothing we can do about your skin, but I think with a touch of makeup it'll look like a tan. Most people born with dark hair lighten it – silly ideas about the perfect Aryan look and all that. Ready!"

She unfolded a sandy-hued towel and beamed. Allison had stood in the doorway, mouth slightly open, while Lee buzzed around gathering towels, scissors, and little glass jars of skin-colored cream. Stepping nervously forward, she allowed Lee to drape the towel over her shoulders position her over the sink basin. She felt absolutely ridiculous with her chin tucked into her chest and her head grazing the faucet. *I hope she knows what she's doing.* Allison shut her eyes tightly.

Lee deftly massaged the liquid into her scalp and worked it through the ends of her hair. Holding her breath, Allison stiffened her neck so that she wouldn't bump against the porcelain sink. Lee sat her on the toilet seat and chatted excitedly while they waited the requisite 20 minutes for the color to set. Allison tucked the towel firmly around her neck and chewed her lower lip. Glancing at her watch, Lee ushered her back to the sink and helped her lean over the bowl again. Warm water cascaded over Allison's face, and she groped for the edge of the towel while Lee rinsed the color out. She nearly groaned in relief when Lee told her to straighten up again. A brisk rub of the towel, and it was done.

"Can I see?" Allison wanted to know.

"Nope." Lee said with a gleeful snap of the scissors. "I'm going to trim your hair first."

With an inward groan, Allison perched on the toilet cover again. *This is exhausting.* Lee shuffled from one side to the other, snipping a bit here, a bit there until Allison nearly fell asleep in her boredom. A loud snip sounded near her ear, and she flinched away from it.

"Now we're done," Lee announced as she set the scissors on the counter.

Allison stood stiffly and wiped the fog from the mirror. Her hair was only a few inches shorter, just brushing her shoulders, and it looked like it would dry to be a golden brown. She touched a damp strand lightly, and the girl in the mirror mimicked her.

"What do you think?" Lee asked in a satisfied tone. "It's 'Burnished Bronze' now. And I think the cut makes you look a bit older."

"Feels weird," Allison answered slowly. "Doesn't look like me at all."

"That's the general idea."

"Does the color come out? Or am I stuck with it?"

Lee bent over to rummage in the cabinet under the sink. "It'll fade in a month or so, and then we'll have to do it again." She emerged with a bag of cotton balls and picked out two of the fluffy things. Rapidly unscrewing a jar of make-up, she dipped the cotton in and peered at the color.

"I think this will work. Allison, could you hang up that towel? I'm just going to dab this around your neckline."

Allison slipped the towel off her shoulders, folded it neatly in half, and threaded it through the towel ring on the wall. Gathering her hair in both hands at the base of her neck, she turned and lifted her chin so Lee could apply the make-up. Lee frowned in concentration. Several deft strokes edged the round neckline of Allison's shirt and her hairline. At Lee's request, she held out her hands for the same application on her palms, between her fingers, and the underside of her forearms.

Finally Lee stepped back, cocking her head critically. "Not bad," she announced. "Good enough to pass a cursory inspection. What do you think of yourself?"

Allison swiveled her wrists to get the full effect of the skin-lightening treatment. She looked in the mirror at her sun-kissed twin. Only her eyes seemed familiar; large, brown, and unsure. A pair of smiling brown eyes drifted into her mind, an oval face framed by long, black hair.

"I don't think I like it," she said, tearing her eyes away from the mirror.

Lee's smile drooped. "Oh, Allison, I'm sorry. But they're still looking for you, so you can't go out looking like yourself. Besides, you won't need a disguise for long; you'll be moved somewhere safe, maybe even out of the country."

"Why can't I stay here with you?"

"This is just a temporary safe house, Allison. If you stayed, they'd find you sooner or later."

Allison hugged her arms across her chest. "I see," she said softly. "I was hoping...."

Lee plunked the make-up and the cotton ball on the sink counter and hugged Allison fiercely. "Don't you dare think we don't want you! Sending you to another house will be the hardest thing we've ever done. I don't want to think about that now."

Lee stepped back and held Allison's shoulders. "Right now I'd like to enjoy having a sister. I'd like to show you the city. Ready now?"

Allison relaxed her arms and nodded. The girls finished putting away the make-up and towels and headed to the kitchen. Sean and Regina were sitting at the table, hands linked together, two cups of steaming coffee before them.

"...and she gave me a great big hug!" Sean finished with a boyish grin.

Regina reached for his other hand and squeezed it, her own face crinkling in a huge smile. They caught sight of the girls, and Sean stood quickly.

"Excuse me, I didn't hear the doorbell." He came forward with his hand extended. "And you are?"

Allison laughed and pushed it away. "Is it really that good?"

"Yes," Sean said decisively. "The best disguises are the simplest ones. What do you think, Regina? From a woman's perspective?"

Regina rose and came around the table, her blue eyes studying Allison intensely. "It is good. I particularly like the hair color, but I think the fake tan is a nice detail. Nobody will give you a second glance." She brushed Allison's hair lightly. "Be careful, honey."

"We will!" Lee grabbed Allison's hand and ran for the door.

"Casually...." Sean's mild caution trailed after them.

Lee slowed to a lady-like walk and courteously ushered Allison out the door. Closing it behind them, Lee led the way down the sunny walk to the street. Allison's eyes shifted nervously from one neighbor to another, but they were all absorbed in their conversations or play.

Lee's old car sat patiently by the curb, its white paint sparkling in the sun. Allison walked casually to the passenger side, her heartbeat soaring with excitement. *Pretend you've been doing this your whole life*, she told herself. She opened the door with a slight fumble and copied Lee's graceful duck and slide into the front seat. Allison shut her door with a sigh of relief. Amidst suppressed giggles, the girls tugged and stretched Allison's seat belt until it finally consented to click in its latch. The engine purred to life, and the little vehicle pulled slowly away from the curb. Allison leaned as far forward as her seat belt allowed to watch the pavement disappear under the hood. She grinned infectiously at Lee.

Once out of the quiet neighborhood, the road took them by places Allison had never been allowed to go: shopping malls surrounded by oceans of cars; tree-studded parks where kids crawled all over playgrounds, teens and adults played any high-energy sports, and dogs loped after balls; and school buildings deserted for the weekend. Everything was painted and cleaned and gardened to perfection.

Allison leaned forward. To her left, above the pristine shops and houses, rose several dark gray buildings. As they drew closer, the facades appeared to be mottled with black stains, and the glass in the windows darkened or broken. The tree-lined sidewalk stopped abruptly, and a crumbling brick wall ran along the road. Hideous curls of barbed wire gathered around a jagged break in the wall. Lee slowed the car as they approached the barricade, and Allison caught the white flash of a sign confronting the street.

"'Warning: Keep Out. This area condemned by the City Council. Trespassers will be prosecuted to the fullest extent of the law,'" Lee read aloud. Turning back to the road, she stepped on the accelerator and maneuvered into the right lane.

"What is that place?" Allison wondered, craning her neck for a better view.

"That was part of the old capitol city before the first Fuhrer took over. He bombed it as an example or warning to the American people, so none of the buildings were safe to use. The Council's been remodeling or pulling down the old city for about forty years now, according to Papa. Those buildings are the last to go."

They turned into the parking lot of a large brick store called Petersen's. Lee nosed the car into a tight space between a van and a sports car and put it in park. The keys jangled like bells as she pulled them from the ignition and toyed with them in her lap, her face remote.

"Lee, what happened to those buildings?"

"Hm?"

"What happened to those buildings?"

"There was a war about 70 years ago. A very nasty one."

"What is war? Why did it happen?"

Lee closed her fingers around the keys, her blue eyes stormy with thought. "Those are questions for Papa."

"Oh." Allison squeezed her hands together between her knees. The girls were silent for a minute. When Allison started to unbuckle her seat belt, Lee covered her hand gently.

"I can't take you in," she said apologetically. "Mom's been bringing me here since I was a baby, and they will want to know all about my new friend. Think you'll be all right out here? We can roll the windows down a bit and lock the doors."

"Yeah, I'll be fine. Go ahead."

"I just need a few things, so it shouldn't take long."

"Go ahead," Allison repeated, hiding a smile from her motherly friend.

After Lee exited the car, Allison found her gaze drawn to the skeleton buildings across the street. The last remnant of a different age. *Why do they have to destroy it? Are they hiding something?* She unlatched her seatbelt, opened the car door, and rested her arms on the warm metal of the roof. With her chin cupped in her hands, she studied the barricade for weak spots. *I could slip through that gap on the left, between the wire and the wall....*

A door thumped shut. Allison glanced to her left and locked eyes with a middle-aged woman leading a boy toward the store. The woman nodded politely and shifted her neutral gaze forward. Allison looked down at the shiny metal beneath her fingers. She lowered herself into the car and shut the door quietly.

The driver of the van returned with a swarm of children in his wake. They each deposited a grocery bag in the back of the van, and the father lifted them into the tall vehicle. It chugged backward out of the parking space and revealed the elaborate brick storefront for Allison's observation.

Lee came striding through the glass doors with a smallish

bag swinging from her fingers. There was a bounce in her step and a dazzling smile on her face, and more than one person watched her progress through the parking lot. She rounded the car, slid into her seat, and triumphantly displayed the contents of the shopping bag. Allison gaped at the lined paper, pencils, pens, and stapler. But the best part was a little book covered with gorgeously detailed paintings of people.

"They're copies of old paintings," Lee said, pleased by the awe on her friend's face. "The pages inside are blank so you can write whatever you want."

"For me? It's for me?" Allison stroked the ethereal images in wonder.

"Yeah. I know you like artwork in our house, and I couldn't resist buying it for you. It sort of jumped off the shelf into my hands."

"I can't write," Allison said quietly.

"I know. I'm going to teach you. How's that sound?"

"Perfect!" Allison beamed and hugged the book to her chest.

Still grinning, Lee started the car and sped for home.

As they entered the house, Sean and Regina jumped up from their seats on the couch and greeted them with a flurry of questions.

"Fine!" Lee answered as she dragged Allison toward their bedroom. "Everything went fine, and we had a great time, and I'm gonna teach Allison how to write, so let us know when dinner's ready...."

The girls shut themselves in the room and went to work. Allison bent over Lee's desk in total concentration as she painstakingly formed the letters of the alphabet. Lee hovered at her side, sometimes reformed a wayward symbol and sometimes just whispered encouragement. But Allison barely heard her, so intent and excited she was.

At last Allison sat back to regard her wobbly alphabets with childish pride. She shook her cramped hand unconsciously while Lee exclaimed over her rapid progress. Allison grinned at the ideas that mushroomed in her mind. *The first thing I'll write will* be a letter to Zip. So he can see *what I've been up to!*

# 15

Lee and Allison spent part of the next afternoon touring the city together. Lee pointed out places of interest as she drove: historic buildings, her favorite places to shop, museums, restaurants, and parks. Intrigued by the secretive nature of the wooded land, Allison had dragged Lee through many winding paths of a public park until their feet ached and complained. Back in the car, Allison drew her feet out of her brown slip-on shoes and sank delightedly into the seat.

"Now I'm ready to go home," she sighed.

"I hope you don't mind if we make one more stop. I need to check in with a contact, see if there are any new developments at the orphanage."

She stopped wiggling her toes to process Lee's statement.

"A contact from the orphanage?" she asked.

"M-hm." Lee smiled lopsidedly. "Might be someone you know."

She glanced over her shoulder and edged into the lightly flowing traffic. Allison scanned the left side of the busy street, trying to guess where might be a likely spot for such a dangerous meeting. The car slowed just before a narrow street that cut between an elegant stone bank and a red brick art gallery. Lee tapped the steering wheel with her thumbs while she waited for a break in traffic. She spun it suddenly, and the car shot onto the cracked and pitted pavement of the side road.

Solid walls of stone and brick rose around them, paring the

sky down to a thin, blue ribbon. Tall, arched windows dotted the faded buildings. Cracked wood doors showed their sad faces every now and then, and occasionally the ancient buildings parted for an instant to show their stair-studded backs and clotheslines dripping with depressed garments.

The alley ended at a fence of warped and rotted boards, and Lee parked the car a few feet in front of it. With an encouraging smile for Allison, she undid her seatbelt and slid from the car. Allison followed her to the corner where the fence joined a crumbling brick wall. There was actually a crack; a sloppily disguised gate clung to the brick by means of a rusty latch. Lee opened the gate slowly, stabilizing it with one hand, and they slipped through.

Stacks of long, naked planks towered over them, stretching as far as they could see from side to side. Saws whined and barked in the distance, and men shouted unintelligibly to one another. The scents of pine, oak, and cherry mingled in the air with tiny shavings of wood that floated like snow.

Allison tugged at Lee's arm and asked, "What is this place?"

"It's a lumberyard," Lee answered in a low voice, "a place where they store and process wood for building things."

"Oh. What do we do now?"

"We wait a few minutes 'cause we're early. My contact will probably come from over there." Lee pointed to the left where there was a barely visible break in the stacks of boards. "We may as well make ourselves comfortable." Then she sat down with her back against the planks and stretched her long legs before her, crossing them at the ankles. She looked up at Allison, an enigmatic smile teasing the corners of her mouth.

"What?" Allison asked.

"Nothing," Lee shrugged, still smiling.

Feeling a bit restless, Allison walked along the lumber pile, one finger lightly tracing the rough grain. *Wonder if the contact is another orphan? Or a guard? Maybe he could tell me about Yanna....* She made it to the end, where the pile stopped abruptly at a chain-link fence, and turned to retrace her steps.

A large, solidly built man strode toward them. Allison

squinted to make out his face, but she could only discern such details as an untucked work shirt and worn jeans. And skin like dark chocolate. *Cuba?* Allison picked up her pace. He stopped by Lee and offered his hand to help her up. She climbed gracefully to her feet, keeping Cuba's hand, and he gently smoothed her hair away from her face with his free hand. Lee turned when she heard Allison approach and shifted to Cuba's side.

The big guy squinted at her, then laughed heartily. "Hey, Allison! You made it!"

"You're Lee's contact?!"

"That's me."

Allison grinned in reply. She walked right up to him and impulsively wrapped her arms around his waist.

"Hey, now," he chuckled as he hugged her with his free arm, "what's this for?"

Suddenly embarrassed, Allison dropped her arms and backed up a few steps. "I'm just glad to see you."

Cuba smiled lopsidedly. "Glad to see you, too. I didn't recognize you at first."

Allison touched her newly-colored hair gingerly. "Yeah, it was Lee's idea. They wouldn't let me out of the house unless I looked different."

"Well, it looks nice. Almost natural. How's my buddy Zip?"

Allison grinned. "Bored. Trying to fix everything in his safe house."

"Ha!" Cuba beamed. "He may be fixin' things now, but if they keep him inside too long he'll turn nervous and take it all apart."

"Cuba," Allison touched his sleeve eagerly. "Have you seen anyone from my group? Yanna, Faye, or Neill?"

"Sure. Came across the girls on the stairs the day I left."

"How are they doing? Yanna particularly. She was sleeping a lot before I left."

"Well, she looked fine. Everyone was kinda tense with all the changes. She and Faye stuck pretty close together."

Relief eased through Allison's mind. As long as Yanna was

walking around instead of sleeping, she might be okay.

"Now it's my turn," Lee demanded, taking Cuba's arm. "You two can catch up after your report."

"Task-master," Cuba said affectionately. "All right then. Official report: I escaped."

Lee jerked as if she'd been electrocuted. "You did not," she blurted in disbelief.

Cuba nodded patiently. "Two days ago my work group had a job at Fat Face's warehouse. We were packin' boxes and loadin' up the trucks, and my buddy David dropped one. The box burst open, and machine parts flew everywhere. Guess he broke something special 'cause Fat Face laid right into him. He had David on the floor, kickin' him in the stomach hard as he could." Memory shadowed Cuba's eyes, and he rubbed his forehead. "Well, I've been holding my temper as best as I can. But I snapped right then. Jumped off a truck an' went after Fat Face. The guys pulled me off him when they got over their shock. He was – his face was all bloody. He was out cold, slumped against a truck tire."

Lee touched his forearm lightly. "It's okay," she murmured.

Anguish twisted his face. "I was gonna kill him, Lee. That ain't okay no matter what he did to us." He looked at the ground. "The guys packed him in one of his own trucks. Figured it'd be a couple hours before somebody found him. They sneaked me out the back o' the warehouse, right under the guards' noses, an' I came here. Mr. Saltzman is a kind man. He told me once if I ever needed a friend to come see him. He set me up with a room in the lumber shed and gave me his old clothes. That's it. That's the end of it."

Lee bent her head, her long hair falling like a curtain around her face.

Allison closed her eyes as an image of Fat Face's bulk leaning against a black wheel, his cruel face bruised and swollen with his own gore, slid into her mind. Anger warmed her blood in spite of the pathetic image. *I wish you had killed him,* she told Cuba silently.

"I'm glad you're free," she said aloud.

Cuba smiled sadly. "Thanks. I feel pretty stupid though. If I'd held myself in check, you would still have a contact on the inside. Sorry 'bout that."

"It's okay." Lee raised her head. "Maybe one of your friends can help us. They know where to find you, right?"

Cuba picked at a button dangling from his shirt. "Yeah, but I wouldn't count on it. Security's been tightened since Allison and Zip got out. Some o' the kids are goin' crazy, startin' fights or challenging the guards. Don't know if they'll ever send out another group, but I'll ask Saltzman to keep an ear open."

"That might help. Cuba, have you found out anything about their plans for the kids? The...um..."

"Extermination? No. They've been taking two or three of us at a time, not even trying to space us out, so I guess it's coming soon. What're the higher-ups gonna do about it?"

"Well, I'll let Allison tell you. Papa himself came over to meet her a few days ago."

Cuba turned back to Allison. "You got to meet the Old Man?"

She nodded.

"That's an honor. I hear he doesn't go out much anymore. What'd he say?"

"He asked a lot of questions. I told him everything about the orphanage, and he said he'd try to rescue all of us."

"Wow!" Cuba whistled. "That'd be something! Wonder if he could really do it."

The whine of the saws changed pitch to a low hum, then went silent. Cuba motioned for them to stay put and jogged to the break in the lumber piles. He was still for a minute, listening, then he came swiftly back.

"They're off work now. You should go before the guard starts on his rounds."

"See you next week?" Lee asked softly.

Cuba stroked her cheek with his thumb, then lightly kissed her forehead. "See you next week. Bye, Allison. You be careful."

"I will. Bye, Cuba."

Lee hugged Cuba tightly, her face buried in his worn shirt,

then released him reluctantly. The girls slipped back through the aging gate and got into the car. Allison covertly scrutinized Lee's face as she buckled her seatbelt. The older girl seemed tense, her face tightened and drawn. Mechanically she fastened her seatbelt, started the car, and backed it into a narrow alley to turn around. It wasn't until they were immersed in heavy traffic that she spoke.

"Allison?"

"Yeah?"

"I never keep secrets from my parents, but they don't know about Cuba and me. Please, don't tell them."

"I won't," Allison promised hesitantly. "But what if they ask me about the meeting?"

"Tell them the truth. Just leave our relationship out of it."

"That doesn't seem right."

"I know," Lee admitted, her voice hoarse. "But there's nothing much to tell them. I met Cuba when another resistance worker sneaked him away from a job site and introduced him as our link with the orphanage. I became his contact, or ferry, and we passed information back and forth. We became friends, and then we became something more. I think I love him, but it'll never come to anything. Cuba has to leave the country. I can't go with him. There's very little chance he could ever come back during our lifetimes." She drew a deep breath and released it calmly. "So there's nothing much to tell them. They would only worry about us."

Allison scratched at her jeans with a forefinger while she tried to reconcile this facet of Lee with the others she knew so well. Something about it made her uneasy.

"I think you're making a mistake," she said at last.

"Probably," Lee muttered. "Probably."

\*　　　　　\*　　　　　\*

"I think you're making a mistake. I am in the best possible position to discover the orphans. It will only take a little more time."

Gunther shrugged his massive shoulders and sipped at his coffee. It was black, boiling hot, and scalded his mouth and throat as he swallowed. *Pain*, he reflected, *is essential to life. Without pain, pleasure means nothing.* He looked at the man sitting across the table from him, toying with his own mug of coffee, and considered his companion's words.

"It doesn't matter. Those are your orders: search the resistance group for someone who can lead us to Papa. And no contact until you find that person."

The operative glanced sideways at the kaleidoscope of sound and movement that was the New Munich Coffee House. Night and day its long room was jammed with customers addicted to its unusual blends of coffee and drawn by its reputation for liveliness. A haze of cigarette smoke curled across the ceiling, and red-shaded lamps descended from the cloud on long, thin stems to illuminate the crowded room. Young men and women laughed and yelled and sidled between the little round tables, staining the air with an unpleasant mixture of heady perfumes and cologne. In the large picture window by the door a three-piece band futilely played covers of the latest hits, the singer's voice lost in the dense noise of a hundred conversations. Gunther closed his eyes. The bold scent of freshly ground beans triumphed over all.

"Strange place to meet." The operative leaned forward to be heard. "Our conversation is not for these ears."

"My friend, you could bring a dozen men here, hatch a plot to assassinate the Leader, and no one would hear a thing you said. So relax." Gunther closed his large hands around his steaming mug. "Now tell me about the orphan. Where is she?"

"Buried. They know information has been leaked, so we've only been told of her presence within the safe house system. Only Papa knows where she is."

"And the boy?"

The operative shook his head. "Same situation. They're taking every precaution to protect those kids."

Gunther looked thoughtfully at the black-lacquered table

top. "Then it would be unwise for you to continue searching for them anyway. Concentrate on Papa. Express your admiration for him and listen to their stories about him. Someone always talks too much."

"What about the orphans? Do you still want them?"

"Oh, we want them. I will take over the investigation."

"You." The operative snorted lightly as he eyed Gunther's massive build. "Are you planning to crash the next meeting of the resistance and demand they give up the orphans?"

"No," Gunther said mildly. "I may have the physique of a prizefighter, but I have also learned some subtlety. You should do the same."

The big man rose abruptly and disappeared in the raucous crowd. The operative drained his cup and considered Gunther's veiled threat as he gazed at the empty chair. He would tread more carefully next time.

And now to work. Now to playact and to listen and to wait.

# 16

Light from the streetlamp crept through the window and stenciled tree branches on the ceiling. Allison lay on her side, watching them sway in the silent breeze. A drop of sweat invaded her eye, and she rubbed at the sting. The old nightmare had returned to destroy her sleep, only this time the masked soldiers had forced Papa to the kitchen floor instead of the dark-haired woman. Allison pushed the cotton blanket off her legs and tugged the lightweight sheet up under her chin.

The little brass desk clock ticked placidly in its sleep.

The silhouetted trees seemed to beckon her into the beautiful night. Allison peeled off the sweat-soaked sheet and padded to the desk. Running her fingers lightly over the surface, she located the smooth plastic of her journal and hugged it to her stomach. She shuffled down the twilit hall, dodged the family room furniture, and slipped out the kitchen doors to the patio. Lifting a folding wood chair from the stack by the door, she set it up at the edge of the stones. She curled her toes against the cold grass and opened the journal to the pages that bulged around a slender black pen.

Moon and streetlight combined to cast an unnatural glow on the blank pages. Allison uncapped the pen, set the tip on the paper, and paused. Wind teased the edge of the paper, then folded it against her fingers. She smoothed it back and held it firmly in place. Then she began to write. Her first memories of the orphanage, the fear that drowned the children there, every nightmare, every act of cruelty she had endured trailed across the pages in stark black ink. She wrote without emotion, as an outsider would describe her memories, connected to them only by the tenuous thread of the word "I."

Dawn warmed the paper to a golden white and sparkled in the newly born words. Allison rubbed her achy neck, forming one last sentence and firmly dotting the end of it. She capped the pen, placed it between the pages, and closed her journal. Translucent angels flew about the cover while richly dressed men and women went about their courtly business, smiled at their children, and struck dramatic poses.

*Who would guess such a beautiful book hides so many nasty secrets*, she mused as she traced the elegant faces.

\*             \*             \*

The day blurred together like a watercolor painting. Allison tripped on rugs and knocked over small pieces of furniture and acquired lovely yellow and purple bruises. Her thoughts floated away when Regina or Lee spoke to her, and she shook her head to ground them again. She tried to help make biscuits at lunchtime but found she couldn't remember how many teaspoons of baking soda she had added to the mixture. The Krueger ladies waved her apologies aside and bundled her off to bed.

She awoke, a little less foggy, just in time for dinner. They were all settling at the table when a furtive tap sounded on the glass patio door. Allison narrowed her eyes, trying to make out the features of their shadowy visitor. Sean jumped from his chair with an excited exclamation and yanked the door wide open.

"Brandon!"

In stepped Zip. His wild hair had been trimmed into submission, and he wore a T-shirt and jeans like a normal teenager. His eyes glittered with suppressed amusement while Sean wrapped him in a bear hug, and he patted the older man's back affectionately. Drawing Sean to one side of the door, he spoke softly to someone outside. Papa shuffled into the light, politely removed his hat, and offered his trembling hand to Sean.

Allison dropped her napkin on her plate and got up, unable to repress a huge smile. Zip spotted her and skirted the two men to greet her.

"Hey, Allison, you look great!" He gave her a quick hug, squeezing hard with his wiry arms.

"So do you! I mean, you look normal."

Zip grinned. "I'll take that in the spirit it's meant. I got your letter. Thank you."

"Why didn't you come sooner?"

"Wasn't safe enough, then I got corralled into helping Papa. He let me roam outside a bit, but he wouldn't let me come here. You realize how protective he is of you? Only he and I know you're with the Kruegers. As far as the others are concerned, you might be in Australia already!"

"Where?"

"Never mind. Point is, he's guarding you very closely."

Regina rose and urged Papa to have a seat at the table, and Lee started gathering more plates and silverware from the cupboards. Papa shook his head.

"Thank you, ladies, but we can't stay. We have some work to do, and we need Allison to come along."

Everyone froze.

"Should I pack her things?" Regina asked quietly.

"No, not yet." Papa patted her hand reassuringly. "We will only be gone a few hours. Would you find your shoes, my dear?" he asked Allison. "And perhaps a sweater. It's getting cool, and we will be mostly outside."

Allison nodded and glanced at Zip. His face was expressionless, a sure sign that this outing was something quite serious. She went to the hall closet for a pair of tennis shoes and a lightweight jacket, leaving the others to question and fuss over Papa. Thrusting her arms into the dark brown jacket and carrying her shoes, she returned to the buzzing group. Zip positioned a chair for her, and she sat down to put on her shoes.

"Will she be in any danger?" Sean asked Papa.

"Yes, my boy, she will." Papa raised a frail hand to forestall Sean's protests. "Now don't fuss. Zip and Will are coming, and they will keep us safe. Ready, my dear?"

Allison stood and nodded. The Kruegers gathered around her for a group hug, but they didn't let go. Allison stiffened as Sean began to pray. Her skin tingled while he spoke, as if someone blew lightly on it.

"Lord Jesus, I thank you for Allison. Protect her tonight. Protect all of them and give them success."

"Send your angels to guard them," murmured Regina.

"Yes, Jesus," Lee breathed.

"In Jesus' name, Amen." Sean squeezed them all tightly with his wiry arms and released them. Allison backed up with a forced smile. *That was weird. I hope they don't do that again.* Lee pushed a paper sack into her hands.

"Dinner," she whispered. "Don't let Zip know about the brownie."

"I won't," Allison promised warmly. "Thank you."

Papa turned slowly, and Zip went to hold his elbow as the old man stepped over the threshold. Allison followed and closed the door behind her with a final, cheery wave to the nervous family. Then she caught up with Papa, cupped her hand around his other elbow. They moved silently through the back yard, ducking under maple branches to reach a slatted gate in the fence. Zip opened it soundlessly and held it for Papa and Allison.

The neighbors' square little two-story was dark and quiet. The trio slipped around one side of the house, each with an eye on the windows. A sudden movement drew a squeak of alarm from Allison. Zip hushed her with a chuckle, and she looked more closely at the window. A gray cat hunkered down on the windowsill, its tail twitching, and eyed them curiously through the glass. Allison shook her head, and they continued through the yard.

In front of the quiet house lay an empty street lit by one flickering bulb. A dull tan car sat at the curb under a dying streetlamp. The driver's door opened as they approached, and a man clothed entirely in black emerged and stood waiting. When they were close enough to speak, Papa introduced this blond-haired man with piercing blue eyes.

"Allison, this is Will, our driver and guide for this expedition."

Will nodded seriously and murmured gruff pleasantries. He turned to open the rear door, gently took Papa's arm, and helped him into the car. Zip and Allison went around the vehicle and climbed in. Allison smiled at Papa as she buckled her seatbelt, glad to share the back seat with him. The engine started with a discreet cough. Will glanced over his shoulder before pulling away from the curb.

"Where are we going, Papa?" Allison asked as they wound through sleepy neighborhoods.

"The orphanage," he answered with a wrinkly smile.

Her heart sped with excitement. "Why?"

"Operation Floodgate begins in one hour. We are going to free your friends."

"Oh, Papa!" she breathed.

Eyes twinkling, Papa reached over and covered her hands with his. "Thank you for your help, Allison. This night's mission is possible only because of you."

Allison drew a deep breath and let it out slowly. "Wow. Okay. Can I help?"

Zip twisted his head to grin at her. "We're the welcoming committee, silly! You have a front row seat to the action."

· "That's right." Papa nodded repeatedly. "We will be stationed less than a block away, waiting to greet your friends and guide them into the night."

An excited cry escaped Allison's throat, and she clapped her hand over her mouth. Papa and Zip laughed outright at her reaction, but Will stared at her through the rearview mirror.

"She doesn't need to come," he said . "You should've left her at home where she'll be safe."

"I think," Papa said quietly but firmly, "you'll find the orphans are frightened and suspicious of adults. They will trust us more readily if Allison is with us. And if something goes wrong and we find it necessary to enter the orphanage, she will be our best guide."

"Brandon has been inside. I'm sure he knows his way around, and the orphans know him."

"Yep," Zip acknowledged. "But most of them think I was there as a spy. And I don't know the routines and protocol like Allison does."

Will retreated behind a wall of silent disapproval. Allison grew silent, too, her joy tempered by his protests. *Is it me he doesn't like or just my presence on the mission?* She cupped her chin in her hand, elbow planted against the door. She smiled at the golden lights flashing past; each one took her closer to her friends. *I wonder if Yanna, Faye, and the others know this is their last hour in that awful place.* She imagined them creeping out a back door, shepherded by faceless members of the resistance group to a dark alley where Allison waited to welcome them to freedom. *Yanna will laugh that silly laugh of hers, and I bet Faye will say something at last. Maybe Papa will let them stay with me at the Kruegers'. We'd all have so much fun....*

The car slowed and turned into the parking lot of a cement professional building. Will switched the lights off and went slowly around the back of the building, parking next to a small receiving dock. He turned the key, and the engine noise dwindled into silence. He turned the knob of a hand-held two-way radio, and heavy static ground at their ears. It coughed and stuttered for a few minutes before he finally switched it off. Through the rearview mirror, Allison watched Will's penetrating eyes assess the shadowy alleys that snaked away from the parking lot.

"All clear," he said softly. "We'll proceed down the alley directly ahead and turn right at the first opportunity. No talking. Stay in single file. Let's go."

Will pulled a black knit hat over his pale hair and opened his door. Allison stepped out, her mouth dry with a cardboard flavor. Raising a finger to his lips, Zip arrested her arm before she could shut her door. He pushed it shut so gently, the click of the latch was barely audible. Will held Papa's arm to steer him down the alley. His head rotated warily from side to side, and there was a visible tension in his back. Zip caught Allison's hand, and the two hurried to catch up.

Will turned and glared at them fiercely. "Quiet!" he hissed.

They stepped gingerly over the cracked concrete as Will suspiciously eyed every door and window they passed. But no doors slammed open, no light burst on them from the windows. They skirted dumpsters and cardboard boxes stacked like towers of wooden blocks. Garbage sprouted here and there and gave off horrendous odors that triggered Allison's gag reflex. She smothered her nose and mouth with her free hand and struggled to breathe around her fingers. Zip squeezed her other hand in commiseration.

The alley ended in another wider, cleaner alley open to the yellow light from the main streets. Will guided them to the right, and they clung to the wall as they drew closer to the mouth of the alley. Motioning them to stay back, close to a rusty dumpster, Will edged forward and peeked around the corner. Suddenly warm, Allison tugged at her zipper with shaking fingers. Papa leaned heavily against the wall while Zip crossed his arms over his chest and almost vibrated with nervous energy.

*This is real,* Allison told herself. *Yanna will be coming down that street in just a few minutes!*

Finally Will turned and beckoned them closer. "Take a look if you like," he whispered. He hunkered down against the opposite wall and pulled the small radio from his jacket pocket. Static hummed like a bumblebee.

Allison slowly leaned her head around the edge of the building and looked down the street. The orphanage looked ghastly in the yellow lamplight. Its tinted windows turned a sickly brown, and the gray concrete took on a sulfurous hue. The large flags stirred a little in the night breeze. All was quiet.

"Not a soul in sight," Papa whispered at her shoulder. "Bless the man who designed these buildings. We have the perfect situation for a rescue!" He winked at Allison, and she smiled at his glee.

A scratchy voice fought through the static. "Come in, Hawk, this is Drill, over."

"This is Hawk," Will answered swiftly with the radio close to his mouth. "State your position, over."

"We're at the back door. Everything's quiet. Is it a go?"

Will peered at the orphanage. "Tide, are you in position?"

"Ready and waiting, Hawk," came a cheerful female voice.

"Taxi, are you ready for your passengers?"

"Been ready, Hawk," a gruff voice answered. "Bring them out!"

Will looked to Papa. The old man nodded.

"It's a go, Drill," Will told the radio. "Repeat, it's a go." He stood swiftly, trained his fierce gaze on the bleak building. Not a muscle twitched in his impassive face, but his fingers tightened around the radio.

"Now," Papa said softly to Zip and Allison, "we've bribed one of the guards on night duty. He'll open the back door for our men, who will sneak into the machine rooms and retract those walls."

"What about the guards?" Zip wanted to know.

"They'll be in their own dorms by now. Did you know there's only one door to their wing? Serious design flaw, as it turns out. Our inside man will lock that door, and they will be unable to interfere even if they do hear anything." Papa rubbed his hands together briskly, eyes aglow with satisfaction. "Nothing could be simpler."

Zip craned his neck around the old man. "And they're coming across the street to us?"

"Yes," Will cut in. "Tide will bring them in groups, and you will take them to the parking lot where we left the car. From there, they will be dispersed to safe locations outside the city."

The four watched the silent orphanage eagerly, their ears alert for the sudden spatter of footsteps. Will glanced impatiently at his watch and muttered under his breath. Allison's excitement dwindled into anxiety as the minutes trickled by. Frowning darkly, Will raised the radio.

"Drill, come in, this is –"

A large truck roared by their position, scattering them into the shadows. Another truck followed, then another, their powerful engines bellowing like bulls. They waited for the noise to die away, but it settled to a low rumble that sounded close to them. Will ran back to the corner, poked his head out for a quick second, then pulled it in. He trotted back and crouched before Papa.

"They've stopped in front of the orphanage. What are your orders?"

Papa blinked several times. "That can't be." He staggered to the street, and Will hovered protectively at his side. Zip and Allison followed to peek around them. Three trucks parked with their tails pointed at the entrance to the orphanage, engines rumbling, while the drivers jumped out and ran to the canvas-covered backs. Teams of uniformed men in shining helmets surged out of the trucks and ran into the orphanage, guns in their gloved hands.

"Hawk!" a woman's frantic voice pleaded over the static.

"Back off!" Will spoke urgently into the radio. "Everyone back off! We've got company out front, and they're entering the building!"

Allison's heart thumped painfully in her chest. She turned her head to look at Zip. His face was still, and his eyes looked dull and hollow. He turned away and walked slowly back to the dumpster to rest his forehead against the rotting metal. Despair wafted from him in waves, but Allison's gaze was drawn irresistibly to the nightmare down the street.

The orphanage doors swung open, and a horde of wide-eyed orphans emerged. The faceless soldiers prodded the dazed children roughly into the waiting trucks. *Yanna!* Allison gasped harshly as she glimpsed her friend's wild hair and tiny frame flitting between the lines of soldiers. *Roman, Neill, Faye....* All the kids from her floor, all the familiar faces of orphans large and small disappeared into the open mouths of the waiting trucks. After what seemed like hours, the last groggy boy was hefted in and the canvas drawn closed. The drivers climbed into their cabs, and the last of the soldiers emerged from the building with long lines of security guards following. The orphanage employees carried suitcases, bags, books, lamps, and other household items. It looked as if they had looted their own quarters. One helmeted soldier waved at the line of trucks and shouted an order before he led the guards away down the street.

Five sets of headlights pierced the night. The first truck turned and roared back up the street, and the rest followed. Allison and her friends flattened themselves against the alley walls as the transports rumbled past. The street was quiet again.

Will raised the radio to his lips. "Mission aborted," he said listlessly to his anxious teams. "Drill?"

"We're here." The words were void of any emotion.

"Follow those trucks. I want to know where they go and what they do with those kids. Over."

"Copy and out."

"The rest of you... Go home."

Very slowly, he switched the radio off and pushed it deep in his jacket pocket. His blue eyes still fastened on the orphanage, he slid to the ground and let his hands dangle limply between his knees.

Papa slumped against the building and whispered, "The children. The children."

Simply unable to believe what she'd seen, Allison continued to watch the deserted orphanage. Maybe it had been a waking nightmare, a horrible vision of the future, and her friends still waited to be rescued. Her blood pounded thickly through her veins, and she thought she could hear the surrounding buildings echoing with her pulse. No, it had all been too real.

"We should go, too," Allison said. She slid one hand over her mouth, unsure of where those words came from.

"We should," Will agreed tersely. He rose stiffly. "Come, Papa. We'd better take you home."

Papa started shuffling toward the darkened end of the ally with Will close behind. Zip pushed away from the dumpster and joined Allison. He laid a gentle hand on her shoulder and opened his mouth to speak, but seemed unable to find words. A metallic clatter caught at her ears, and Allison glanced back to see a group of black-clad soldiers pour into the mouth of the alley. She squeaked in alarm.

"Will!" Zip's voice lashed the air.

The mission leader took one look and threw Papa over his shoulder before he broke into a run. Zip and Allison sprinted after him, close on his heels. He turned suddenly into a narrow, reeking lane that conducted them to an open square of pitted concrete. Five unlit alleys opened into it. Will hesitated for a fraction of a second before he chose the most unfriendly-looking one to his right. The little group dodged piles of refuse, stagnant puddles, and rusty dumpsters. Allison stepped on something soft, and it groaned a curse. She bit back a scream and struggled on. The distant clatter of guns and the muffled stamps of booted feet faded away into the night.

The four shot suddenly into the parking lot where they'd left the car. Will called to Zip to open the doors, and he gently deposited Papa inside before sliding behind the wheel. Allison and Zip were only half-way in when Will started the car and began to back up. They slammed their doors hastily, and Allison gripped the handle as she fought for air. Will spun the wheel, his fierce gaze burned through the rear window as he careened backward into the street. Yanking the car into drive, he stomped on the gas pedal. They lunged forward, and Allison's head jerked back. Lights and buildings flashed by at crazy angles. She closed her eyes against the vicious onslaught of motion.

"Everyone okay?" Will asked tightly.

"Allison?"

Sobs built in her chest until they burst out of her mouth like harsh bird cries. Hot tears and mucus gushed down her face to meet them. Grief shook her until her head rang with it.

"Allison!" came Zip's panicked voice. "Will, stop the car!"

"No!" Papa shouted back. "Get us to the Kruegers! Slow down a bit, and get off the main roads!"

Papery hands stroked her arm, and an unstable voice spoke soothing nonsense as the car moved away from the brilliant lights and settled into a gentler pace. Allison drew her knees up, wrapped her arms around them and rested her throbbing head against them. Her body still shook under the force of the violent sobs, but she didn't feel it. The others talked urgently, almost angrily, but she didn't hear them. Grief tore at her with its jagged teeth. She shrank away from it and found within herself a soft gray world of neither pleasure nor pain, only silence.

# 17

Allison lay listlessly on her side and contemplated the sun-starved walls of Lee's room. *They are gray.* She rolled to her back and angled her head for a view of the curtained window. Only a feeble bit of sunlight came through. *Everything is gray.* With a sigh she rolled back to stare at the wall. *Everything is gray.*

"Allison?"

She turned her head. Lee bent over her, face drawn and eyes puffy from crying.

"I didn't hear you come in," Allison said tonelessly.

Lee sat gingerly on the bed and circled Allison with her arms. Laying her head against Allison's shoulder, she whispered, "Will was just here. All your friends are gone. I'm so sorry."

Allison sought the grayness of the wall and immersed herself in comfortable numbness again. For long minutes Lee held her and breathed raggedly against her own grief, then released her and left the room. Allison drowsed, occasionally alert to a shift of shadows or click of the doorknob. Voices blended into the static of her mind, but she paid no attention to their words. A guttural sound jarred in her ears. She moved to her back, suddenly curious.

Papa sat in the desk chair next to her bed. He twisted a soft gray hat in his fingers. Sorrow hung heavy on his face, and his round shoulders hunched close to his thin chest. Lifting his eyes, he met Allison's gaze, and something of a smile touched his mouth. He cleared his throat again.

"I was hoping you'd come back," he said a little unsteadily.

She shifted a little, let her cheek sink into the pillow.

Papa folded his cap and drew a deep breath. "I have a story to tell you, if you're up to listening to an old man ramble."

"Okay," Allison agreed quietly.

Papa looked wistfully toward the window. "This used to be such a beautiful country, my United States of America. Such freedom, such inventions, such wonderful cities. This used to be the capitol city, you know, but they've destroyed all her grand old buildings, all but a few...."

Papa turned back to her. "I was about your age when my we Americans went to war. The newspapers cried out against injustices in lands we'd only heard of in history books, and politicians gave speeches over the radio to persuade us to stand by our allies across the ocean. But we were reluctant to take up our guns so soon after a war that had ravaged much of the world. Many didn't believe the refugees' horrible stories of a monster named Adolf Hitler. So we waited. Our allies were buckling under ferocious attacks. The stories were confirmed by important men rescued from Hitler's purges. So my freedom-loving country stood by its promises and sent its soldiers off to fight Hitler's armies."

Papa coughed into a handkerchief, folded it neatly, and tucked it in his shirt pocket.

"For a year everything went well. We sank their U-boats, took back the supply lines, and reclaimed ground on the African continent. We planned a massive invasion on the coastline of occupied France with the hope that a concentration of our forces could break Hitler's Reich." He smoothed the hat on his lap. "It failed. We lost the main part of our expeditionary force on those rocky beaches, caught like rabbits in barbed wire fences and mine fields.

"From that point everything went wrong. England, our strongest ally, lost most of its leaders and munitions factories in a series of bombings and was forced to surrender. We Americans retreated to our own shores to strengthen our defenses. Though we were strong and vigilant, and guarded by two oceans and a good ally to the north, they came."

Papa's eyes faded as he looked deep into his memories. "We were betrayed from within. Even in America, Hitler's passionate speeches had found sympathetic ears. Those American Nazis sent false orders to our outlying ships and planes, left their posts at crucial times, and launched an offensive against our own leader, the President. Most people escaped harm, but much of our capitol city was destroyed by long-range bombs. Remnants of the military fled west, fought the invasion as best they could, but they were beaten by sheer numbers. Hitler swept them into the sea as one would sweep dry leaves from a porch.

"My little town, like many others in America, was at first untouched by the war. Change came to us gradually; first the soldiers came to declare new laws, then the foreign governors and their police to enforce the rules. One by one, our laws were replaced by Nazi policies. The Jews and the loud-voiced dissenters were taken away, and national Germans moved into their houses. We learned to speak German quickly since they refused to acknowledge the English language.

"One summer I played baseball with my friends every day, going home only to eat and sleep. The next I was sent to a Hitler Youth camp. We watched films of the Fuhrer's speeches, read of his struggles and successes, marched like soldiers, and learned by heart the tenets of Nazism. Oh, we had fun as well. They seduced us with membership to any kind of sport we liked, special classes that sped us through high school, any kind of job we wanted, and the sense that we were bettering ourselves and our country. Most of us exchanged our names for Germanic ones to cement our new allegiance.

"That is how it began for me. I left my little town in the Midwest to be a filing clerk in the newly rebuilt capitol. The Government Security Department offered jobs on all levels with the promise of promotions. It seemed just the place for an ambitious young man." Papa smiled wryly. "I was terribly curious, too. When my manager wasn't around, I liked to peek in the folders to see what the Germans were up to. One day I found a quick sketch of their plans for my Jewish countrymen, for Christians, for anyone who opposed the new government. It sickened me. For days I couldn't bring myself to return to work, so I called in and pleaded ill health.

"A concerned friend came to check on me, and I told him what I'd read. He was just as horrified as I. And angry. He wanted to stop the GSD from carrying out their plans. Organized resistance movements had done much to hinder Hitler's armies in Europe. Why couldn't we do the same? We formed that group, he and I, and swore to fight against the tyranny that held sway over our country. We used our jobs to tap into the brain of our enemies and ruin their plans. Over the years we quietly recruited those sympathetic and courageous enough to help us. On the surface we married, had children, worked hard, retired, and grew old. We smiled at our conquerors while we rescued their victims."

Papa cleared his throat noisily. Allison found herself sitting up with her hands knotted tightly in her lap. Reaching for a delicate porcelain cup on the bedside table, Papa took several sips and cradled the cup in his hands.

"Ahhhh," he sighed. "Excuse me."

"Papa...." Allison began.

The old man raised a hand. "No, my dear, let me finish. I have survived this horrible system. And in spite of its murderous attempts, so have you. You must cling to life, and by your very existence you will triumph over this system of hate. Remember the past. Carry it with you and share it with those in other countries. And you must tell them your own story."

"Are you sending me away?" Allison's voice cracked with pain.

"In a few days, yes," Papa said gently. "You cannot stay longer without endangering yourself and the Krueger family."

"But you're sending me out of the country."

"You have grown up in a world that hates you and has done nothing but try to harm you. Many would become bitter and resentful and full of hate themselves. But you are compassionate and brave, a beautiful legacy of peoples now gone from this earth." Papa reached for her hand and grasped it tightly. "Don't you see, my dear? Children are our hopes and dreams, our greatest treasures. I am sending you away because you are the child of my heart, and I can't let them destroy you."

He squeezed her hand between both of his and stood up with care. Allison stared at him mutely, grief flooding and choking her throat. Unfolding his hat, Papa set it carefully on his head and smiled sadly at her.

"Good-bye, my dear. May God bless and protect you; may he smile graciously upon you and give you peace."

Holding the back of the chair, he turned awkwardly and hobbled to the door. Allison watched his bowed back disappear and swallowed hard as the door closed softly. She let her eyes travel around the room. *This is my home,* she thought wistfully. *This is where I learned to write and think and live. I love the Kruegers. They're my family. Oh, Papa, you're asking me to tear my own heart out!* Her tears puddled in the folds of the cream-colored blanket. They flowed until there was nothing left but tenuous tranquility.

Wiping her eyes with her fingers, Allison remembered the precious words Papa had given her. And the mission. She peeled back the covers, slid out of bed, and padded to the desk to search for her journal. She found a corner of it peeking from under a science textbook and drew it out. She went to the window and pulled the curtains aside, and the late afternoon sun poured in. She rubbed at the dazzling orange images it seared on her eyes, then sat cross-legged on the floor. Mouthing the words to herself, she scrawled Papa's story in the last few pages of her book. She shut the book firmly when she had finished, but a horde of frightened orphans marched across the street of her memory. *Be our voice. Write our story, too,* they seemed to say.

Allison opened her journal again. She licked her dry lips and set her pen tip to the paper.

She forced herself to relive that night, every nasty odor that wafted from the dumpsters, every pale face that disappeared into a truck, every footfall of the race to safety, every jerk of the car as they sped through the light-crazed city. Ruthlessly she focused on every detail until she had exhausted her memory. The orange glow of the sun dwindled into grayness, and it was done.

*Another ugly piece of truth,* Allison thought grimly as she shook her aching hand.

"Allison?" came Lee's tentative voice.

The blonde-haired girl leaned into the room and examined her with a blend of fear and hope. Her face was blotchy with old tears, and dark rings stamped the skin under her eyes. Allison smiled wanly as she laid aside her journal and tucked stray tendrils of hair behind her ears. Relief washed over Lee's face, and she came to sit by her friend.

"Are you all right?"

"No," Allison admitted. "I feel old and tired inside."

Lee inched closer and placed a comforting arm around her shoulders. "I'm sorry about your friends."

Allison leaned her head back against Lee's arm. "I was going to rescue them. I was supposed to help Yanna and Faye and Neill get to safety, but I had to watch them ride to death instead."

The girls watched a rosy blush of light creep over the walls, wrapped in their thoughts and emotions. The silence and Lee's company had a soothing effect like Faye's tranquil spirit, a thought that sent a twinge of pain through Allison's heart. She rested her forearms on her legs. Lee emerged from her reverie at Allison's abrupt movement and asked, "What did Papa say to you?"

"Is he still here?" Allison picked absently at the beige carpet.

"No, he left with Zip just after he talked with you. He told us you'd be fine, but he looked so depressed and worn out. Resigned. What did you two talk about?"

Reluctantly Allison met her friend's inquisitive blue eyes. "He said I have to leave."

"Oh." Lee's eyes clouded over. "Did he say when?"

"No, just that I have to leave the country soon."

Lee wrapped her arms over her tummy. "I guess I shouldn't be surprised. But it still feels like my family's being torn apart...." She straightened suddenly, indignant. "You're leaving something out, aren't you? What else did Papa say?"

"He told me his story. How the war changed this country. What it did to him and what he decided to do." Allison pushed her fingers deep into the carpet fibers. "He told me I'm precious to him. And he wants me to tell everyone in other countries his story and mine."

"He's right," Lee said softly. "You are a wonderful mix of many races. You're all that's left of their history, their traditions...."

Allison's fingers froze as an ocean of faces swarmed through her mind -- faces fierce as hawks, softly rounded with youth, seamed like tree bark, or daintily curved in feminine shapes. Their skin was a harmony of black, olive, coffee, and honey tones beneath dark hair of every imaginable texture. Lively eyes gleamed above high cheekbones, arching or wide noses, and full lips. Each was fully alive in its expressions of hope, amusement, thoughtfulness, and sternness.

Allison sucked in a deep breath as Lee continued.

"....So however much we want to keep you, we have to send you where you'll be safe."

"I never thought of it that way," Allison said, still blind with the images of her forebears.

Lee leaned forward to capture her eyes, her silky hair cascading over one shoulder. "It's not just your background. You are an incredibly sweet person, and we all love you very much. And God loves you more than all of us put together."

"God and his love," Allison echoed tonelessly. "If He loves us so much, why did He let my friends be carted away to be killed?"

Pain darkened Lee's eyes. "I don't know. I don't know."

Silence grew between them, wrapped them in dozy warmth and dust motes.

The door opened with a slight creak to reveal Regina's drawn face. She relaxed visibly when she saw Allison sitting peacefully on the floor with Lee. She came to join them, and the girls made room for her in the window nook. She knelt by Allison, folded the girl in her arms, and rested her cheek on Allison's head. Allison inhaled the mingled scents of fresh-baked rolls and dish soap that emanated from Regina's clothes. She nestled peacefully in those motherly arms.

"I thought we'd lost you," Regina whispered against her hair.

"I wanted to be lost," Allison admitted softly. "But I think I'm glad to be here now."

Regina rubbed her shoulder with her thumb. "I wish you could be a permanent part of our family."

"Me, too." *You have no idea how much I wish that.*

"The plan is to move you to another house tomorrow. You'll stay there a few days before your guide arrives to lead you out of the city."

"Why can't I stay here until it's time to leave for good?"

"Our neighbors have been watching us rather closely. Papa thinks all that activity the other night made them suspicious. And Robert, your new host, lives on the other side of town, closer to the harbor. It's for the best. It'll be all right," she spoke reassuringly.

"It's too fast," Allison protested.

"I know." Regina cocked her head to see Allison's face. "But I'm so grateful for the time we've had with you. We'll miss you."

Lee brushed at her eyes with her fingertips. "Mom, you're gonna make me cry again. Let's do something." She climbed swiftly to her feet. "Let's pack a bag for Allison. She'll need some clothes and toiletries at least."

Lee walked purposefully to her closet. She rummaged in one of the dark corners and emerged with a small brown suitcase. Allison reached up, found Regina's wrist, and clung to it while Lee hunted through the room for Allison's belongings. They were quickly swallowed by the leather bag, and there seemed to be plenty of room in its belly for more. Lee frowned down at the open-mouthed bag, hands limp at her sides.

"It seems like there should be more," she said, bewildered. "You shouldn't be able to fit your whole life in one suitcase."

*I wish I could take my whole life with me,* Allison told her silently, *but your family won't fit in there.*

# 18

The traffic light glowed red, and Lee stepped on the brake as they approached the gray car idling in front of them. Allison rested one arm on her brown bag and leaned against the car door. She cupped her chin in her hand and stared mournfully at the light. *I wish they'd all turn red and freeze there.* She sighed through her nose. *Silly! A few red lights won't stop the plan. You're leaving, and that's the end of it.* Gazing at the neat lines of vehicles at the intersection, she wistfully recalled her last minutes with Sean and Regina Krueger.

"Have you got everything you want, Allison?" Regina asked as she placed a paper bag of baked goods in the little suitcase. Brushing a wispy tendril away from her face, she glanced around the living room as if she wanted to stuff it in, too. Allison sat on the couch next to her bag with a tight ball of tissues crumpled in her fists.

"I don't know," she answered lamely.

Sean came out of the library with five books in his hands and, head on one side, attempted to read the titles as he walked. "I can't remember which ones you wanted to read, so I grabbed all of the European history and a volume of Robert Frost." He corrected the angle of his head and offered her the books.

"It was the third one, I think," Allison answered as she fingered the worn blue fabric. "Are you sure you want me to take it?"

"Oh, yes," Sean smiled. "They're very easy to replace. Can

you fit the fourth in as well?"

"There's plenty of room, honey." Regina relieved him of the chosen books, lifted the paper bag, and placed them neatly on top of the clothes. "What are we forgetting?"

"Toiletries," Lee answered, holding up a white cosmetic bag as she came in. "You left them in the bathroom."

Regina took the plastic case and wedged it in next to the baked goods. She was about to close the zipper when both Sean and Lee stayed her with frenzied exclamations. Sean cut around the easy chairs to the kitchen, and Lee jogged back down the hall. Allison squeezed the tissue and then opened her fingers to watch it expand slowly.

"Here, Allison."

She glanced up. A thick pocket-sized book lay cupped in Lee's hands.

"Your Bible?" Allison asked, stunned.

"One of them," Lee corrected her. "Will you take it as a gift from me?"

Allison hesitated. Lee's expression was such a blend of eagerness and anxiety that she felt unable to refuse. Allison gently lifted the holy book from her friend's fingers and set it on top of the others.

"Thank you, Lee."

"And here's a little gift from me." Sean leaned around his wife to tuck a crackling bag next to the Bible. "The best chocolates in town – dark with caramel filling."

Allison touched the candy and murmured her thanks. Folding her hands around the crumpled tissue, she stood and looked searchingly at the Kruegers. Regina's smile wobbled a little, and Sean's shoulders slumped just a bit more than usual. With a bittersweet smile, he put an arm around Regina's shoulders and reached for Allison with the other. She ducked her head, opened her own arms, and the little family encased her in one long hug. Lee's hair tickled her right ear as she joined the circle.

Sean began to pray in a broken voice. Allison only heard the raw emotion behind the words, so absorbed was she in trying to memorize the tone of his voice and the mixed scents of roses and pancakes wafting from Regina. They released her slowly, both suspiciously wet around the eyes. Lee sniffed as she turned to zip the suitcase and carry it out to the car, leaving the front door open behind her. Allison watched her hair blaze as it caught the morning sun. The grass, the sidewalk, the snug little house across the street looked so crisp in the early light, they seemed like something conjured from her imagination. *No, it's all too real*, she thought sadly. She looked back at Sean and Regina.

"Thank you," she said softly. "I love you."

Allison gave them each a quick, fierce hug and walked swiftly out into the surreal brilliance. Her senses caught on every chirp of the birds, the clean scent of the grass, the promise of autumn in the air's cool touch. She avoided looking at the house as she swung open the car door and dropped into her seat. With shaky hands, she latched the seatbelt and picked up the suitcase to cradle it in her lap.

"Okay," she said resolutely.

Lee started the car and inched forward. Allison's will faltered, and she looked over her shoulder. Sean and Regina stood in the open doorway, arms wrapped tightly around each other. Her eyes locked on their figures until she lost them among the thick-leafed trees and orderly houses....

The red light winked out abruptly and green blinked on.

The gray car leaped ahead, and Lee followed at a more sedate pace. Allison hugged the suitcase to her chest. In the park on her left, a soccer ball spun through the air and bounced off one of the players' heads. The men jostled each other as they chased the grounded ball. It launched onto the sidewalk before a line of neat Victorian style homes. Allison blinked, then a time-pocked concrete wall materialized to race alongside the street. Beyond it rose the dead monuments of another culture. *My culture.* It flashed across her mind like lightning, and struck a longing in her heart.

"Stop!"

Lee jerked. "What? What's wrong?!"

"Nothing, just pull into Petersen's." Allison tapped frantically on her window as the store appeared on the right.

"Okay," Lee breathed and swung the wheel.

It was a tense car that turned into Petersen's parking lot and slipped between two pick-up trucks. Lee shut off the engine and stared anxiously at Allison, but her eyes were riveted on the bristling wire across the street.

"What are you thinking?" Lee asked.

Allison focused on her friend. "I want to go into the condemned quarter."

"Now?!"

"Right now. When will I have another chance? Please, Lee...."

Lee lowered her head onto her arms and muttered something under her breath. Allison glanced around the parking lot. Busy, everybody absorbed in their own affairs. Finally Lee sighed and sat upright. She turned her head to look at the barricade and spoke tonelessly

"Walk at your normal pace. Don't look around a lot or someone will know you're up to something. Try to act like you're just going into another store."

"What do I do if someone sees me?"

"People see what they want to see, but sometimes you can influence their thoughts with your attitude. Be casual and confident."

"Okay." Allison released her seatbelt, fingers shaking in anticipation.

"Don't be too long," Lee advised. "No more than 20 minutes, all right?"

"All right." Allison smiled reassuringly before she stepped out of the car.

"Watch out for the barbed wire...."

The door shut on the last part of the sentence, and Allison strode purposefully toward the busy street. *Just doing something totally normal and boring*, she explained mentally to the people passing by. No one took any notice of her as she approached the curb. An icy calm spread through her. She stepped into the street, dodged the oncoming traffic, and slowed to a walk before the menacing barricades. On closer inspection, the prickly wire had rusted to the rotted wood of the fences. Allison followed the curves of wire until she found a careless gap between two barricades. She squirmed through, walked quickly on the cracked pavement until the noise from the street ebbed away. Then she stopped and looked around.

The tall buildings stood mute in the warm sun, like trees in the grip of winter. Their windows turned a dull stare on the world, neither seeing nor blind. Doorways gaped at the emptiness. Grass and dandelions flourished in the broken road – nature reclaiming its territory. The cold pall of terrible secrets hung in the air, and silence throbbed a warning to any who might open their mouths to remember.

"But you can tell me," Allison whispered. "No one will find out."

She wandered up to the nearest building and peered through grimy glass, searching for something that would speak to her. There was nothing -- no papers littering the sidewalks, no bullet holes or glass fragments, nothing but the effects of time. *Is this what Hitler's soldiers did? Sweep away everything but its bones?* Someone obviously wanted the past forgotten. She continued on the decayed street.

A couple blocks away, Allison found a three-story building with letters still visible above the doors. Stone fought against the vandal time to hold on to the word. Beneath the sign, heavy wood doors were propped open as if stuck in a perpetual yawn.

Curious, she went in and found herself in a huge room. The ceiling rose to a majestic height supported by a network of metal beams. Dust-coated shelves sagged forlornly against the walls and each other. Rows of them marched through the room and lined the walls, spotlighted by mammoth windows set close to the ceiling. Allison meandered down the wide aisle that split their ranks. Treading softly on the graying marble floor, she followed the aisle to the next room.

It was an empty space with long windows set almost

seamlessly in the curving outer wall. Between four graceful columns, intricate swirls and lines formed a circular pattern in the floor. As she moved to stand in the center, Allison's eye caught on an incongruous element in the flowery border. Intertwining vines almost concealed the letter "e." She turned slowly and found a sentence in the outer circle of the design. To her dismay, it was in the English language. She recognized "I," "over," "to," and other simple words, but the rest were unfamiliar.

Allison sat cross-legged in the bath of light and studied the lovely weave of word and vine. If she closed her eyes, the letters might rise from their resting place and rustle like leaves around her. The air felt heavy with the weight of their precious secret.

"Thank you," she said to the still room. Turning slowly, she meandered back through the enormous main room. Allison rubbed her eyes. The warmth of the sun rendered her mind sluggish and hazy. She stopped in the middle of the room and threw her head back to look at the towering ceiling.

A sense of despair engulfed her, the despair of a highly-advanced civilization. No, more than that -- the loss of something beautiful, ideal, and true struck down suddenly and without hope of resurrection. Allison shuddered and ran in a panic to the open doors, her feet pounding like a drum in the stillness. She drew a deep breath as she emerged into the mild sunlight. She felt foolish for reacting to the atmosphere like a little kid.

*Still*, she encouraged herself, *I don't think anyone could stay long in that place.*

Arms crossed over her chest, she turned and walked slowly back toward the gap in the wall. She imagined the sidewalks bustling with families going shopping and men in perfectly cut suits going to and from work. They walked beside her, and some of them smiled or nodded or said "Excuse me" as they passed. Everyone was happy and relaxed and kind to each other. A society that used freedom as its foundation, a society that shunned no one. Allison sighed as the wind turned her fanciful thoughts to dust sifting across her path.

She stooped and plucked a large dandelion from a hole in

the sidewalk. Cradling it in one hand, she trailed her other hand lightly along the face of an ancient storefront. The new city hummed cheerfully, obliviously, beyond the wall. Reluctantly she went back to civilization, back to the world that condemned her as it had condemned this old corner of her people's world. She turned around and gazed wistfully at the old quarter. *I could stay here. But they would find me when they come to destroy it.* She laid her hand on the last building in a farewell gesture and took the last few steps to the opening in the wall.

A swift glance from side to side showed nobody was interested in an adolescent girl sliding delicately out of a forbidden zone. Allison breathed a sigh of relief and dashed across the street. She approached the car to find Lee hunched motionless over the steering wheel. Allison whipped open the passenger door, scooted in, and gripped her friend's shoulder. Lee jumped a little and turned an agonized face toward Allison.

"It's okay," she croaked. "I was only resting and praying. You can let go now."

Allison dropped her arm and muttered an apology. "You scared me. Why do you have to pray in weird positions?"

"It was comfortable.... What did you see?"

"Not much. That place is completely dead and empty. "Almost." Allison carefully set her dandelion on the dashboard and smiled sadly at Lee.

"It meant that much to you?"

"Yes. Thank you."

Lee studied her face carefully. "Okay."

On the way to the rendezvous, Lee peppered Allison with questions about the condemned quarter. She was surprised that the structures themselves were left intact, nearly untouched for no apparent purpose. In her preoccupation, Lee almost rammed into the back of a van at a stop sign, so she steered the conversation to a less engrossing topic.

"While you're at Robert's house, you can write letters to me and he'll see they're delivered. So we can communicate for a few more days at least."

"That's wonderful," Allison said fervently. "I will miss you so much, and it'll help to at least write you."

"I'll miss you, too." Lee shot her a watery smile. "We're almost there."

She indicated a run-down gas station with a nod. Its sign had faded from red to orange, and the lettering was barely readable. One decrepit pick-up truck sat at a pump and guzzled gas while the driver stared off into the distance. The girls drove around back and found Zip in a small silver two-seater. Lee pulled up beside it and shifted into park.

Allison moved sluggishly. Flower. Bag. That was all. All of it easily gathered in two hands. She clung to it with wooden fingers.

"Got everything?" Lee asked.

"Yeah."

"Need any help?"

"No."

"Okay." Lee exhaled. She engaged Zip as soon as her head cleared the roof of the car.

"You look civilized. Did those people make a gentleman out of you?"

"Thanks," Zip said dryly. "They certainly tried, and I love 'em for it. Hi, Allison."

He favored her with one of his best grins before enfolding her in a nice hug. When they parted, she noticed new dark smudges under his eyes and an unusual tautness to his skin.

"Good to see you, kid," he said warmly.

"And you," she answered cautiously. "What's wrong?"

"Just the inevitable. I'm not here to be your chauffer; I'm going into exile with you."

"Oh." Sympathy welled up in Allison's heart. "I'm sorry. But I'm glad you're coming with me."

Zip nodded. He yanked open the miniscule trunk of his car and tossed Allison's suitcase next to a battered black duffle. She crossed her arms, slightly hurt by his childishness. He slammed the trunk shut with the palm of one hand and turned to face the girls with a tight smile.

"I hate good-byes, so I'll just hop in now."

"Bye, Zip," Lee called to his back. "Take good care of yourself and Allison."

He raised a hand in acknowledgment and shut the door. Lee turned back to Allison with tears pooling in her eyes.

"I wasn't going to cry," she said as she futilely brushed at the tears. "Thanks for being my sister for a while."

"Thanks for taking care of me. I love you."

They gave each other one last hug, and Allison stared over Lee's shoulder at the crumbling blocks of the gas station in an effort to maintain her composure. She patted Lee's back and stepped away.

"Remember to write," Lee reminded her as she walked with her to Zip's car.

"I will. Say bye to Cuba for me."

"Okay."

Allison bumped her head on the frame as she climbed in. Tears slipped free and transformed Lee into a watery image of sky blue and pale gold against the sun. Then she was gone. Allison rested her aching head against the warm glass of the window and stared vacantly at the busy road ahead.

"The Kruegers are great people, huh?" Zip observed. He swung the wheel expertly and stepped hard on the gas pedal to slide into a niche between cars. "I've got a lot of respect for them. They're always willing to do whatever's needed. Biggest hearts I've ever come across."

"When'd you learn to drive?"

"Changing the subject, are you? Okay. A couple years ago when I worked at an appliance place. There was an old car in back of the shop. I tinkered with it, sorta learned the ropes, but it wasn't drivable. The guy who owned the place taught me to drive his car so I could pick up parts for him."

"Is it hard to learn?"

"No, just takes practice." Zip shot her a quick glance from the corner of his eye. "What is it you're trying to avoid?"

"Pain, I guess."

Allison waited for him to comment, but he just nodded and focused on the road. She squirmed under the prodding effect of his silence and decided to bare her heart.

"I've lost all the people I care about. I lost Yanna and Faye and the others to death. I've lost the Kruegers and Papa because my background endangers them. Cuba's leaving, too, and I have no idea where he'll go. Everyone I love becomes a painful memory. Maybe it would be better not to love."

"That's no way to live. If you get all depressed and hide in your shell, you've let those ba-... um, those bullies win! We may not have a golden future, but we have to go on fighting. We've got to clean our wounds and be willing to take new ones so we don't die inside. You can't let it drag you down."

Allison smiled wryly. "At least you take your own advice. I forget you've been through a lot of pain."

"Yep. Have to take it in stride and go on."

Leaning her head in her hand, Allison looked at Zip curiously. "What are your wounds? Losing your parents? Betrayal?"

"I prefer to keep those private," Zip said somewhat stiffly. He glanced at her, softened a bit, and continued gently, "They're adequately healed now, but I don't like bringing them up again."

"Okay, that's fair."

"And if you ever want to talk about your troubles, I'll be glad to listen. For the next few days, at least. After that we're off to fight this battle from a distance, and I have no idea if we'll even stay together."

Allison was thoroughly confused. "You've been pushed out of the resistance, and now you're talking about fighting from another country. Even though you don't think we have much of a future. What do you want to fight for?"

"Hey, no defeatist talk from you, miss," Zip ordered playfully. "I know all that. The future I'm fighting for isn't mine. The world isn't going to change overnight, but it won't ever change if we give up on it."

"You're not as selfish as I thought you were." Allison clapped a hand over her mouth.

Zip laughed goofily at her blunder, a good shoulder-shaking laugh that nearly sent him into spasms. Allison instinctively put a hand out toward the steering wheel in case he lost control. A car passing them in the left lane honked indignantly as they swerved a bit. Zip waved carelessly at the motorist, still chortling. She shrugged and placed her hand back in her lap. She considered it an achievement to make him laugh even if she had no clue what was so funny.

They finally pulled to a stop in a middle-class neighborhood on the north end of the city. Allison eyed the slightly shabby houses doubtfully, wondering what kind of people lived in them. Zip hopped nimbly from the car and snatched their bags from the trunk before Allison could offer to help. She rubbed her arms nervously as she looked up and down the quiet street.

"You sure it's safe to park here and walk right up to the front door?"

"Yep," Zip answered as he presented the little suitcase to her. "Robert has a lot of visitors, so we don't look a bit suspicious. And he'll take care of the car for us. C'mon."

They traveled carefully over the uneven sidewalk leading up to a white house with neat gray shutters framing the two front windows. Zip stepped up on the concrete stoop and knocked on the smooth gray door. The man who opened it seemed to belong there, Allison was pleased to note. Mild brown eyes regarded them from a round face framed by wavy brown hair. His white button-down shirt and brown dress pants were immaculate, and his patent shoes gleamed with polish. He smiled when his eyes lighted on Zip, and he greeted the young man with a warm handshake.

"Hey, Zip. That was some disappearing act you pulled," he said as he held the door for them. "Had me worried for a while. Well, welcome to my humble abode. Is this the famous Allison? I'm Robert Stokes. Congratulations on a successful escape."

His big hand was a bit clammy, but Allison managed not to pull back too soon. "Thanks for letting us stay here."

"No problem, no problem." He smiled and waved away her thanks. "A bachelor like me is always glad to have company. Let's get you settled. The guest room's back here, and the bathroom is right next to it...."

Robert's voice trailed off as he led them into a sparsely furnished living room and down a narrow hallway. Allison picked up her own bag and followed Zip and Robert to the back of the tiny house. She bumped repeatedly into the walls and stepped on Zip's heels twice. The hall led straight to a bedroom furnished simply with a bed, tall dresser, and nightstand of golden oak. Linen-colored curtains framed the window, and the glow of the sun warmed the white walls and bedspread.

"Not exactly a palace," Robert's voice broke into her thoughts, "but I do keep it up for guests like you. The dresser's empty, Allison, so you can go ahead and put away your things. This room is sacred, and we gentlemen will not enter without your permission."

"Where is Zip sleeping?" Allison asked as she dropped her bag on the faded coverlet.

"On the couch in the living room. I'm afraid there are only two bedrooms, and ladies should have the most comfortable accommodations."

"Thank you."

"Well, come on out for dinner when you're ready. I'm afraid I didn't have time to cooks, so it's only take-out from a restaurant. Zip, let's get you settled. I have plenty of blankets...."

Robert chattered on about the accommodations as he propelled Zip out of the room. Allison sank wearily onto the bed, placed her wilting dandelion on the nightstand, and rummaged through her bag for the chocolates. The bright wrappers crackled soothingly, and the rich smell neutralized the odor of cleaning solutions. *Almost sterile*, Allison thought with a sniff. *Like the nurse's office.* She scooted back so she could lean against the headboard and stretch out her legs. Biting into a truffle, she chewed without really tasting it. Chocolate was small comfort for an aching heart, but she reached for another. Her fingers encountered a different kind of paper among the smoothly wrapped candy. She drew out a square of white stationery and unfolded it.

My dear daughter,

Besides these chocolates, I wanted to give you a gift, something precious. The most valuable thing I have to share with you is Jesus. Please, don't stop reading if you are uncomfortable with the idea of God. He loves you so much. He lived and died for you, Allison. He crushed sin and broke death's power so that you could be with him. If you read nothing else in the Bible, read the book of John, one of the men who knew Jesus intimately. If you remember nothing else, hold onto this: all who cry out to Jesus will be heard and saved. That is the sweetest, most precious gift. And it's yours.

With love,
Sean Krueger

Allison folded the note slowly. She glanced at the corner of the Bible peeking out of her bag.

*Maybe.*

# 19

**B**reakfast at Robert's house was certainly a far cry from the Krueger tradition of fun messes and savory smells. A nauseating smell of scorched food assailed Allison's nose as she halted in the doorway. The kitchen counters were bare but for a stack of dirty mixing bowls by the sink, utensils bristling from the top. At the range, Robert poked at something in a frying pan with a stained spatula. A black apron was tied snugly around his crisp blue shirt. He hummed tunelessly to himself until he caught sight of Allison gaping at him.

"Good morning! Did you sleep well?"

"Yes, thank you," she managed. "What are you making?"

Robert gazed sadly at the frying pan. "It ought to be French toast, but it doesn't seem to be turning out well. I'm afraid I'm not much of a cook."

"Hey, Robert!" Zip called from the living room. "Got a minute?"

"Be right there!" He handed the spatula to Allison with an apologetic smile. "Would you mind taking over?"

The would-be chef untied his apron while he walked, and Allison stepped up to the range. She poked at the blackening toast, scooped it up, and looked around for the trash can. Under the sink. She dropped the burned toast in and moved back to the range. *Too high, Robert*, she corrected him mentally as she turned down the gas. Then she moved in to rescue a pan of scrambled eggs, adding salt and pepper and turning up the heat. *Thank goodness he only made two,* she thought as she dipped the soft bread in the egg mixture and placed it gingerly in the hot pan. Allison patiently worked between the two pans until she had a heap of golden toast on a large platter and the eggs solidified and fluffed up nicely.

She rummaged through the stuffed shelves of the refrigerator for some kind of fruit. *Apples.* Gathering three of the mottled red fruit from their basket, she washed and sliced each one precisely into eight pieces. A quick review of the cupboards revealed a small selection of dishes, but she found three matching plates. Allison served up her breakfast and carried it to the white-painted table by the window. Easing herself into a chair with a sigh, she started on the eggs.

Robert and Zip entered with appreciative noises and went to the counter to investigate the covered dishes. They served themselves and joined her at the table. Robert eyed the French toast appreciatively.

"How on earth did you salvage this meal?" He took a bite and chewed rapidly. "S'wunnerful!"

"Just changed the heat settings," Allison replied simply.

Zip wasn't his usual energetic self. His eyes looked sleepy and vague, but he cocked his head in a familiar way when he noticed Allison's scrutiny.

"Nice robe," he commented.

"Nice hair-do," she shot back.

Allison matched him stare for stare as she snuggled deeper into the floral garment. It was comfortable even if it was several sizes too large. Zip chuckled at her indignant manner and attempted to smooth his cowlick. An image of another breakfast, perhaps ten years in the future, flitted through her mind. She and Zip moved around each other in a sunny, comfortable kitchen as they cooked breakfast together. He smiled intimately at her with those mischievous eyes.... Warmth flooded Allison's cheeks and ears, and she ducked her head.

"So," Zip turned his attention to his host. "Mind if I use the computer? I promise nothing will happen to it."

"Yeah, sure. I'm working 'til five, so I can't entertain you. Maybe we'll do something this evening." He glanced at the wall clock. "I better get going. See you later!"

He set his empty plate in the sink and trotted to the front door, tie flapping around his neck. It closed behind him with a creak, and Allison watched through the window as he hurried down the sidewalk to his car.

*I hope he'll be too busy to entertain us*, Allison thought. *I don't think I'd like it.* Zip must have been thinking the same thing because he pulled a silly face.

"Board games," he said disdainfully. "Checkers."

"Oh. Well, I'll clean up the kitchen. What are you gonna do?"

"Check on the car and try to make contact with our guide, the one who's supposed to get us to the harbor."

Allison rested her chin in her hand. "Do you know where we're going?"

"Nope." Zip pushed back from the table and got up to deposit his dishes on top of the others.

He went off to change his clothes and soon left through the back door. Allison plowed through the dirty dishes and reorganized the cupboards as she put them away. The overstuffed drawers proved to be a challenge, since there was no other place for Robert's massive collection of utensils. Allison sighed in exasperation as she inspected three long-handled whisks. She finally found an old coffee can and arranged the superfluous utensils in it like a bouquet. After wiping down the counters, she left the kitchen with the satisfaction of a job well done.

Zip had still not returned.

Not even the gentle ticking of a clock relieved the silence.

Allison retreated to her bedroom. She lifted her bag to the bed and dug through it for a wrinkled green shirt and a pair of gray pants. She fingered the cuffs of the pants. They had been cut and shortened with meticulous little stitches in order to fit her. She changed quickly, grabbed pen and a notepad from the nightstand, and curled up on the bed. Head propped on her left arm, Allison scribbled letters to the Krueger family over five sheets of paper.

*I hate it here*, she wrote feverishly, *but it's not really bad. I've just gone from a real family and a home to a bachelor's blank house. I wish you could visit. That would make everything better. Almost.*

Allison sat up and folded the letters into envelope shape. One for Sean, one for Regina, and one for Lee. She hopped off the bed and rummaged through her bag for her folder of writing supplies. No envelopes.

She padded to the living room to find Zip lounging comfortably at the small desk in the corner. He had just turned on the computer and begun to browse through a magazine while he waited for it to boot up. Allison rounded the ugly plush sofa and stepped over a pile of car and computer magazines.

"Hey, there." Zip glanced up with a welcoming smile.

"Hi. Do you know if Robert has any envelopes? I want to send some letters to the Kruegers."

"Sure." He leaned down to open the bottom drawer on his left and lifted out a box of long envelopes. Allison looked around the room for a chair, spotted a square stool serving as a coffee table, and dragged it back to the desk. She perched at Zip's left side and quietly stuffed and addressed her envelopes. She tapped them into a neat pile. The computer was ready, and Zip's nimble fingers moved swiftly over the keyboard.

"I saw Will," Zip told her with his eyes glued to the screen. "He gave me an update on our escape plan...."

"Which is?"

"We leave tomorrow night."

"Oh." She fidgeted nervously with the hem of her shirt. "What're you doing?"

"Will also gave me clearance to perform a special hack. I'm searching for a way into the GSD system that won't get us arrested. And when I'm done with this, I'll take a peek at these babies." He tapped two microchips sitting next to the mouse.

Allison straightened up. "Hey, are those from Memory

Square?"

"Uh-huh." Zip grinned lazily.

"You took them?!"

His grin widened.

Allison gaped at him in disbelief. Zip laughed at her and returned to the task at hand. The computer screen displayed an "Access Denied" message and stated in lofty terms that the information he sought was classified. Zip groaned and buried his face in his hands. He emerged from his disappointment to mutter nasty imprecations at the complacent screen.

He tried several number combinations to bypass it, but none worked. Grumbling under his breath, Zip plucked a black disk from his shirt pocket and shoved it in the open mouth of a drive. He cracked his knuckles as the machine whirred. A smile hovered around the corners of his mouth. The screen wavered for a second before righting itself.

"Gotcha," he whispered gleefully.

"What did you do?"

"I used a program that unscrambles number passwords. Now, let's pick their brains."

He scrolled down a list of files, pausing at a few cryptic names. The few he opened looked like legal briefs from the GSD hierarchy. Allison inched closer so she could read them, but she was mostly disappointed by a series of inconsequential law interpretations. Zip skipped down and stopped at a file called "Project O."

"This looks promising...."

A highlighted picture of the human anatomy appeared with several paragraphs of notes beside it. The words heading the page made Allison's mouth go dry. The Project Orphan file contained a complete list of the atrocities inflicted on kids like her as well as the details of the extermination plan. She traced the words as she read them in a shaky voice.

"'Separated from parents at birth..... surgically altered to prevent reproduction.... drilled in necessary studies in order to be useful to society.... Termination will begin in waves of 1,000 every year beginning with the oldest in January and end in August....' What do they mean by 'surgically altered?'"

"It means," Zip said grimly, "That you can't have children. By ruining our reproductive systems, they've effectively wiped out the 'inferior' races."

Allison was frozen to her seat, too horrified to cry. Sorrow caught in her throat, seared her lungs with its soundless agony. She felt again the despair that saturated the walls of the old quarter. For an endless minute she seemed made of stone herself.

"Allison."

She clenched her hands to stop the trembling and choked back her burning grief.

"What?" she croaked.

"I can find out exactly what happened to our buddies from the orphanage."

"No. They died. That's enough."

"Okay. I can bring up your file if you want. We can find out all about you, who your parents are, if they're alive. I'll need your ID number."

Allison methodically rubbed her knees with trembling fingers. "A160434."

Zip mouthed the numbers as he punched them in. They both gazed anxiously at the screen and nearly jumped when glaring white text appeared on a black background. Allison leaned forward until her nose was inches from the monitor and her stool creaked a warning.

"I'm fifteen," she announced, her insides melting from their stone-like state.

"And mostly Italian, Greek, and Polish," Zip pointed at the paragraph outlining her antecedents. "Your family's got too much tainted blood for the goons' comfort, but I think it's great. Those were very fascinating cultures in the old days. In fact, the Greeks were building colleges and conquering the world while the German tribes were still using stone tools and speaking to each other in grunts."

"Wow," Allison breathed.

"Yeah, no kidding. Let's see…. You were taken from your mom at age three, and she was placed in a labor camp."

"But she could still be alive…." Hope sparked in her mind. "What about my dad?"

"Um, nothing about him. Don't know if that's good news or bad."

Allison's hands locked on her knees as a new fear wormed its way into her heart.   "Zip, if they've killed all the kids, what will happen to the adults? My mom?"

He looked at her, wordless, then rapidly tapped at the keyboard. Allison's knees began to ache from the grip of her fingers. She released them and clenched her fingers tightly together in her lap. *Please, please….*

"Allison." Zip's voice sounded alien.

"What?"

"Allison…."

His voice wobbled, and she reached for his shoulder as if she could steady him.

He turned his head to meet her gaze. Horror darkened his eyes.

"They're gone, too."

She stared at him, simply unable to absorb his words.

"And not just in this city," he continued in a whisper. "All the people in the labor camps and orphanages across the country have been wiped out."

Allison dropped her hand limply. Her addled brain attempted to put together the sounds that had emerged from Zip's mouth, but they refused to make sense. She opened her mouth but found she had nothing to say.

"I'm so sorry about your mom." Zip leaned forward, arms open to wrap her in a hug.

*My mom.* A face shook itself free from a curtain of silky black hair. Eyes deeper than dark chocolate smiled warmly at her and –

Allison spun off the stool and walked blindly into the knee-high corner of the coffee table. She cried out sharply, bent over her injured leg, and found she couldn't stop the howling pain. Zip touched her back lightly with an incoherent murmur. She straightened swiftly and whipped around to face him.

"Why?" she shouted raggedly. "What did any of us do to them? What? She was so sweet and gentle! She never hurt anyone!"

"Allison—"

She slapped his hand away. Tears streaked down her flushed cheeks like molten silver, and her chest heaved with fury.

"We never did anything wrong! We don't deserve this! Who gave them the right to kill us off?"

Zip let his hand fall to his side. Unshed tears shimmered in his eyes.

Too wrapped up in her rage to notice his wounded expression, Allison whirled and wrenched her injured knee. She snapped her teeth together and stalked to the sofa. With both hands clamped around her leg just above the kneecap, she lowered herself to the cushion. She rocked back and forth as waves of pain broke over her.

Zip stood rooted to the middle of the room.

Allison's breathing slowed, and the hot pain ebbed away. At last she leaned wearily against the sofa's comfortable back and angled her head to look at Zip.

"I was hoping," she said quietly, "that we would find each other, and she would pull me into her lap just as she does in my memories. And just hold me." Her gaze dropped to nothing. "Silly, but I was hoping."

Silence settled heavily about them. Zip slid his hands into his jeans pockets and let his head droop. Spent of all emotions and words, Allison melded into the couch. She jumped a little when Zip suddenly turned and went back to the computer. He typed furiously, shoulders set in a hard line. She blinked drowsily.

\*                     \*                     \*

The front door burst open, and Robert's voice called a booming hello. Allison jerked out of sleep. She rubbed her gritty eyes gently with her fingertips and blinked at the late afternoon sun creeping across the tan rug. Zip turned sideways to shout hello, his face masked with a cheerful demeanor. Robert came in to set his briefcase on the single easy chair and smiled at Allison.

"Hi. They let us out early today." His smile faded as he studied her face. "Something wrong?"

She fought the last vestiges of sleep away and found a clear answer. "Banged my knee."

"On the coffee table, I'll bet."

She nodded.

"I should replace that thing. I do that all the time." He loosened his tie, and went to peer over Zip's shoulder at the screen.

"Are you hacking again? Will this reflect on me in any way?" he joked.

"Maybe," Zip admitted. "I don't know how closely they're watching these files, but I think I disguised our entry well enough."

"That's my buddy." He patted Zip's shoulder. "Who's the victim today?"

"The GSD and Project O."

Robert's face turned an awful pasty white. His eyes bulged, and he opened and closed his mouth like a fish.

"Hey, it's okay," Zip patted his arm sympathetically. "It's only marginally stupid. You wanna go lie down for a bit? You don't look so good."

"Sure, yeah," Robert sputtered. "I think I'll call my doctor. Something's going around the office, and I probably caught it. I'll call my doctor."

He staggered toward his bedroom, discarding his tie and bumping into the walls as he went. Zip shook his head pityingly as he turned back to the keyboard.

"Is he all right?" Allison wondered.

"Yeah. He has a heart attack every time I do something risky with his equipment. Doesn't usually get that pale, though. I want to save this Project O stuff for Will. Where does Robert keep his disks?" Zip poked through the desk drawers and came up empty-handed. He swiveled to face her. "How's the knee?"

She flexed it carefully "Getting better."

"Good. Allison, would you go ask him where the disks are? And tell him the updated plans. We should start packing soon."

She eased off the couch and winced at the pain that rippled through her knee. She slowly navigated the cave-like hall and trailed to a stop in front of a closed door, reluctant to disturb her sick host. His voice rose in a sharp whisper, and Allison caught a word that nearly made her heart stop. She turned the doorknob softly and cracked the door open.

"I *know* I'm breaking orders about contact, but your subtlety has landed you in hot water…. Will you listen to me?! That untraceable hack? It's him! Zip is prowling through your system with total freedom…. They just landed in my lap!…. You told me *not* to contact you….Well, I couldn't stay home and babysit! You pay me for information, not to play daddy to those brats…. No, you don't understand! They'll be gone tomorrow…. Fine. You better arrest me, too, so they don't get suspicious. When will the squad be here?…."

Allison sucked in her breath and eased the door shut. She flew back to the den. She dodged the mess Zip had made during his search, pulled up by the desk, and grabbed his shoulder.

"Relax," Zip said, drawing back. "We're doing fine. I found a di—"

Allison cut him off. "Robert called the GSD. They're coming, and we gotta go now!"

"You're saying *he's* the mole?" Zip stiffened, his face vacant as the news registered. She shook him a little so his eyes focused on her again.

"Are you sure?"

"Dead sure, but feel free to ask him. Sounded like he'd be happy to kill you himself."

Zip held up a hand. "Just hang on a minute, okay? Pull out the disk when it's finished loading."

He paused only to grab a few tools from his bag before he ran lightly down the hallway. Allison shifted her weight nervously. With one eye on the street, she pocketed the letters. Every second she expected the GSD to pull up in their black vans and encircle the house. Long moments of silence dragged by, then came the sharp echo of nails biting into wood. Muffled bellowing and thumping followed. Zip emerged and vaulted the sofa. He snatched Allison's arm just as she retrieved the disk.

"You were right," he said curtly. "Grab the microchips and the letters — let's go!"

He propelled her to the back door and jerked it open. They began to run.

They pushed through a neatly trimmed hedge and barged through gates in the white-fenced back yards of the neighborhood. They surprised several children splashing in a pool and an elderly couple half-asleep in their deck chairs. Allison almost stepped on a long-haired dog snoozing in the shade of a giant bush covered with clumps of purple flowers.

"This is too open!" she yelled to Zip. "Can't we hide in the middle of the city?"

"No!" he shouted back. "Have to head north — gotta get out now!"

At the end of the block, beyond a particularly thick hedge, rose a stately line of maples and oaks - a park. Zip raced alongside the prickly bushes as he looked for an opening. He scooted sideways through a small gap and ground to a halt. Allison bumped into his back, and he pushed her back with a motion for silence. The two stared across the street.

It was a beautiful park, with neatly trimmed green spaces between the clumps of trees. Wrought iron benches reclined gracefully along the gravel path that wound into the shade and beyond their sight. A shadow shifted slightly behind a flowering bush. A flicker of sunlight gilded something hard, something dark and metallic. Allison drew in a sharp breath, and her eyes swung down the street. There, the outlines of a large black van bulged from behind a pick-up truck.

Zip swore harshly. "Go back!" He spun around, eyes burning with anger and fear, and shoved her back through the hedge.

She tore across the grass. One swift glance over her shoulder - a round black object bobbed and weaved and glared sullenly at the sun. *Helmet.* Panic coursed through her veins, and she found in it a fiery energy. Zip passed her, took the lead again, and nudged her into a driveway. They dashed recklessly across the street, up a cracked concrete driveway, and squeezed between the squat garage and the peeling yellow house. Zip snatched a lawn chair as they passed the deck and cast it against the chain-link fence that towered over them. He stepped on the seat and swarmed to the top of the fence. With one leg and arm clinging monkey-like to the other side, he reached for Allison.

She stretched one hand up blindly. Zip gripped her wrist tightly and urged her to climb as he hauled her up with surprising strength. She rolled awkwardly over the ragged edge, and Zip let her dangle a second before releasing her. Allison landed on her tailbone but was up in a heartbeat, the smack of boots on concrete in her ears. Zip shifted his weight over the fence and hit the ground rolling. He wiped at the sweat streaming down his grim face as he gained his feet.

"We'll lose them in the city."

Allison nodded, relieved. Zip started jogging. He led her south in a zigzag pattern until they found a major street that ran straight as an arrow into the market district. As it widened from two to four lanes, more people appeared on the sidewalk, strolling languidly in the autumn heat.

"Newspaper stand coming up," Zip said briskly. "Watch the headlines."

The little stand's sides were hidden beneath newspapers and garishly colored magazines. The pages fluttered every now and then so that the booth looked like a giant bird settling its plumage. The two fugitives slowed to a fast walk as they passed it. Allison's eyes flicked over the newsstand, catching on random words.

*War in Brazil.... Fuhrer Grunwald's Speech.... Economic*

*Stability.... Gottlieb's New Policy Revealed.... Serial Killer Arrested....*

"See anything about us?" Zip murmured in her ear.

"No. Did you?"

"Nothing. I guess they're keeping this game under wraps."

"Why?"

"The GSD has already announced our escape once. Wouldn't do to remind the public that we're still at large. They'd rather announce our capture -- makes them look better."

*I guess that's comforting*, Allison thought doubtfully.

Pedestrian traffic thickened into slow-moving clumps of shoppers. Zip and Allison squeezed past groups of women with brightly colored shopping bags ballooning from their hands. Excited chatter rose and fell amidst the rumble of traffic moving steadily north to the suburbs. The sidewalk stretched out beneath a patchwork of shade and sun; some storefronts kindly extended an awning for overheated shoppers, and others baldly refused them any shelter. Tangy citrus scents drifted into pungent onion, and over both triumphed the bold aroma of coffee and the dense, sweet smell of baked goods.

"Zip?" Allison said tentatively, her stomach in sudden agony.

He squinted at the lazily setting sun. "Soon."

She swallowed at the memory of her last meal at Robert's.

The small grocery stores and coffee shops gave way to jewelry and appliance stores, then a squat apartment building and a procession of stately old houses. Above their peaked heads skyscrapers loomed, their top stories hazy in the liquid gaze of the sun. Cars and trucks parked bumper to bumper along the street, at rest for the night. Zip and Allison approached the yawning trunk of a sedan, and Zip glanced keenly at the overstuffed bags of groceries inside. Without a pause in his stride, he leaned over and lifted a bottle of orange juice from the nearest bag. Allison's mouth swung open. He coolly untwisted the cap and passed the bottle to her.

She looked incredulously at him. "You stole it."

"They've stolen far more from us," he said absently. His eyes roved over the next intersection.

Allison put the bottle to her lips and swallowed a little guilt with the juice. *Never again,* she told herself firmly. Zip reached for the bottle as she lowered it and took a generous swig. He capped it and passed it back to her for safekeeping. She took it reluctantly, and Zip looked at her for a minute before returning his attention back to their surroundings.

A line of affluent-looking people curled neatly out the door of an aging brick building with gracefully arched and latticed windows. Above the open door floated a peeling, gilded sign announcing the place to be "Armand's." Zip eyed the restaurant with the same attentive expression he'd given the bags of groceries. A few of the lady patrons adjusted their holds on their purses and edged closer to the building as they passed by. Allison focused on the street sign ahead, on the actual function of breathing. *Just ignore them. Just keep your pace.....*

"Very promising," Zip pronounced happily.

He strode by the last elegant window of Armand's and the insurance company next door, with Allison trotting steadily at his side. At the next intersection of well-kept streets he turned right and right again at an alley marked "Deliveries Only." Not a scrap of litter desecrated the pavement, though the requisite dumpsters were present, and not a stroke of graffiti stained its walls. Zip whistled approvingly.

"This is definitely the place to eat. Come on, let's see what we can find."

Images of a darkened alley rolled through her mind.... stark, wide-eyed faces.... The thunder of a dozen trucks roared in her ears.... Allison folded her arms over her suddenly pounding heart. *This isn't the same alley. They don't know we're here. It's okay. It's okay.*

"I was thinking," Zip said, "of taking a peek in those dumpsters."

"Dumpsters?" Allison faltered, returning foggily to the present.

"Yep." He approached the two metal containers sitting by the back door of Armand's. "Restaurants are notorious for throwing out perfectly good food. Simply because a customer can't finish his meal, and they don't want anyone eating the 'contaminated' stuff, they toss it in the trash."

With an impish smile he lifted the lid of the nearest bin. Allison shifted her feet, then took a hesitant step. *And what else do they put in there?* she wondered as she remembered the broken glass and tattered cleaning rags Regina had deposited in her trash bin. Zip thrust an arm eagerly into the wide mouth of the dumpster and withdrew two white paper bags stamped with golden A's. He let the lid close with a crash and examined the contents of one. Allison deliberately absorbed the details of the area as she came closer, wallpapering her hideous memories with images of this alley.

"It's good," Zip announced. "Come sit down."

He rounded the dumpsters and sat with his back to the wall, legs stretched carelessly before him. Allison sank wearily at his side and set the juice bottle on the ground between them. The edges of the weathered bricks jabbed at her back through her thin cotton shirt, but she just laid her head back against their cool faces and welcomed the rest.

"Common folk call these 'doggie bags,'" Zip lectured as he produced clear plastic containers of tenderly grilled chicken and soft rolls wrapped in white napkins. "Somebody couldn't finish his dinner, asked the waiter to pack it up so he could take it home, and forgot all about it. Lucky for us. Like some cooked carrots? Wish they'd thrown in a fork and spoon for you, but they don't usually."

Allison accepted the offerings with a little shake of her head. "I don't care. Thank you."

Zip shrugged as he popped the lid off a limp salad. "Not much to it. Probably couldn't have done better if I'd swiped a whole bag of food from that overloaded car." He looked at her, eyes suddenly serious. "I won't do it again if it bothers you. But we won't find much to drink in dumpsters."

"Okay," she answered around a mouthful of chicken.

They ate the rest of their meal in silence. The sky melted into tranquil shades of rose and lavender, and they craned their necks to watch the coming of night. It was a strange sort of darkness, one that hovered just above the city's glow and refused to show its rich depths. Allison slid her shoes off and yawned hugely. Zip scooted down and folded his arms behind his head.

"Think you'll be able to sleep here?" he asked.

"Tired enough to. Wish it wasn't an alley, though."

"Yeah, know what you mean."

Allison curled up on her side facing the dumpster and pillowed her head on one arm. Dark rust spots blurred together with her tears, and she closed her eyes to their hypnotic dance.

# 20

**B**ANG!
Allison's eyes flew open. A slim, wavy-haired man stood over her, brushing nervous fingers across an impeccable white apron.

"You kids better go before the chef arrives," he said, not unkindly.

"Right. Thanks," Zip rasped.

The man nodded and went through the back door of Armand's.

"Ungh," Allison moaned. Her bones felt rusted into place. They protested like old machinery when she pushed them into a sitting position. She swept clinging strands of hair away from her eyes and glanced skyward. It was a pale dawn, slightly golden and mildly warm. The ever-present hum of the city droned vaguely in the background.

She pushed the heels of her hands against her eyes as yesterday took her by storm. Letters, Project O, their crazy run through the suburbs, thirst that sucked at every pore of her body.... The death of her mother.

"Where now?" she asked aloud.

Zip cracked his bones into compliance as he stood, twisting his neck and back and arms unmercifully. "Don't know. We just keep moving for now. Any juice left?"

"Uh-huh."

"Drink a little now. Save the rest for when we're really thirsty."

Allison probed her mouth with her tongue and found that it stuck to every surface in its quest for moisture. *When could I possibly be more thirsty?* She unscrewed the cap with clumsy fingers and splashed a little into her mouth. Zip took it from her and offered his other hand to help her up. She straightened slowly, groaning all the way.

"Old woman Allison." Zip flashed a quick grin before lifting the bottle to his mouth. He took a swig and capped it, eyes narrowed on the entrance to the alley.

"Let's get moving."

And move he did. Allison cast a sideways glance at him, mystified by his easy gait and the comfortable way he carried his head. *We both read the same horrible files yesterday. We both scrambled all over the suburbs. We both slept on the same pavement. Doesn't any part of him remember?*

Zip turned right at the junction of alleys, leading her into a narrow street of suspicious-looking character. He turned this way and that, seemingly at random, though his unwavering step declared him fully master of his way. Allison craned her neck at every intersection to search for the hidden street signs or landmarks that guided him. She could pick out an odd-looking door here or a startling planter of geraniums there, but she had to give up at last. Eventually she forgot her aches and pains in the confusion of streets and the hunger that chewed the walls of her stomach.

"Can we stop for food?" she asked at last.

"Sure. Pick a dumpster."

Allison eyed the rusty, grimy bins ahead. Hunger quieted into a vague nausea as she caught a whiff of their contents. "No, thanks. Can we take a break?"

Zip squinted at the metallic blue sky. "We've been walking for a few hours. Guess we could sit down for a few minutes."

Allison angled for a relatively clean bit of pavement and plopped down. Zip sat next to her and offered the juice bottle. *Less than half left.* She took just enough to fill her mouth. The liquid to pushed at her cheeks before she swallowed. She waited for Zip to drink a little before she spoke.

"Why aren't we taking the main roads? We could hide in the crowds and get out of town faster, couldn't we?"

Zip shook his head firmly. "The goons know we haven't made it out to the north. They'll tighten their circle now, concentrating on the east and south. Which is roughly the direction we're heading."

"But they have no clue where we are...."

Zip smiled gently at her. "Did you know I have a record with the GSD? The orphanage wasn't my first encounter with them. They know me. They know how I operate. Back streets and alleys were my playground as a kid. I've always come here to hide. But outside, the GSD has all the advantages. And all they have to do is wait for us to come out."

He leaned his head back against the wall, eyes fastened on nothing. Allison studied his tense profile. In spite of his bleak words, his brain was racing down every possible avenue of escape. *Hopeless*, she told him mentally. *It's hopeless, but you won't admit it.* Shifting to one hip, she drew the letters she'd written to the Kruegers from her pocket. She smoothed the wrinkled envelopes in her lap.

"I guess I should get rid of these," she whispered.

She pressed one hand to the concrete to leverage her way to a standing position, but Zip grabbed her other wrist. Allison frowned at him in confusion. He stared at the letters.

"We have that disk," he said. "It's still in your pocket."

"Ye-es....."

Zip's eyes gleamed. "Don't throw those away. They may find us, but we have something to do first."

"What do you mean?"

"The disk!" he said impatiently. "I forgot about the disk. I forgot about Robert. Idiot!"

Zip let go of her, sprang to his feet, and strode back the way they came.

"Zip?....." Allison clambered up and jogged after him.

"Utterly stupid," he chastised himself.

Allison flapped her arms in frustration. "What?!"

"We can't just sneak outta here. We have information Papa desperately needs: the files on that disk and the identity of the mole. The entire resistance movement in this city will be wiped out if we don't get that information to him."

"Oh!" Allison sashayed around a murky puddle and scrambled to catch up with Zip. "What are we gonna do with it? What are you thinking?"

"I know a man in the area who used to work with the resistance. We'll give the disk to him, tell him about Robert the Traitor." He shot a lopsided smile at Allison. "He could deliver your letters for you."

Allison clutched the envelopes so tightly they curled in half.

"We gotta move fast, though." Zip squinted up at the sun. "Time is not our friend."

*     *     *

Allison leaned against an aging wood fence and picked nervously at the splinters. She glanced over her shoulder as Zip tested the gate with his fingertips. It creaked like an old man clearing his throat. Zip screwed up his face. Allison held her breath. It swung open without further complaint, and nothing worse than silence followed.

"Wait here," Zip murmured.

He crept into the yard and was gone.

A bit of white paper somersaulted against the fence and rested there. One corner nodding lazily in the light breeze. Somewhere down the alley a well-oiled gate closed with a dull thump. Allison's head jerked toward the sound. Nothing. No one.

*Quit it,* she scolded her jumpy fingers. She dropped a bit of wood and shook her hands in disgust.

Zip sidled through the gate, easing it shut behind him. Then he turned and put his back against it.

"So?" Allison whispered eagerly. "Was he there?"

"No. I left the disk, your letters, and a note. Checked the garage in case he left the car. Nothing doing. Would've been nice to have a vehicle."

"Yeah," Allison sighed. *More walking.*

"Ready to go?"

Allison nodded her acquiescence and stooped to pick up the empty juice bottle. They headed toward the end of the alley.

"Where are we heading now, Zip?"

"East. Across the street."

"Oh. Can't we wait 'til night? They'd have a harder time spotting us."

"Normally that's what I'd do, but we're racing against time now. We could still make the ship before she sails if we keep moving."

Something rustled behind them. Allison whirled around. A cat's striped tail disappeared through a slightly open gate. Zip looked at her quizzically.

"You're really jumpy."

"Yeah," Allison grimaced. "I don't know why."

"You dropped the juice...."

"I got it." She forestalled him with a raised hand and bent to pick it up. She straightened just as a gate slammed back on its hinges. Five armed men in black cargoes burst through it. The leader yelled as he spotted them, and the group charged down the alley. Allison clutched at Zip's shirtsleeve. He grabbed her wrist, and they dashed out of the alley. Zip barreled across the street without glancing right or left. Allison instinctively threw an arm over her head as brakes screamed angrily and metal bit into metal.

A terse command sounded from their left. The rear doors of a black van parked along the street swung open, and a team of black-clad men jumped out. Zip kept his heading and poured on the speed. They ran through a jungle of lawn furniture, bushes, and fences, but the heavy footfalls of their pursuers thumped persistently behind them.

Allison clenched her teeth against the pain exploding in her chest as they sprinted across a four-lane street. Sirens wailed dangerously near, and she glanced to the right to see a large dark truck bearing down on them. Zip turned sharply, pulled her across an intersection into a crowded parking lot. They ducked and weaved around the cars and got partway across the lot before Allison's legs gave out. She tumbled to the pavement with a ragged cry.

Another siren howled triumphantly.

She pushed against the hot pavement, fighting to get back on her feet, but her exhausted body refused to cooperate. Zip darted back to her side and tried to haul her up. She opened her mouth to urge him on, but he suddenly toppled to the ground. A booted foot crushed him against the pavement.

"Don't move! Don't move! You are under arrest!"

GSD operatives swarmed around them and roughly searched their clothes. Allison pressed her cheek against the asphalt and shut her eyes against the black-visored helmets that hovered over her. Icy metal clamped around her wrists. She sent up a silent cry of despair.

*Jesus, help me....*

# 21

Four walls of seamed concrete formed her cell. She sat on a smooth concrete floor and looked up at the concrete ceiling. Everything was hideous, blank gray except for the stark white bulb that had become her sun, moon, and stars. Under its reign there was no sleep, no time, no comfort.

Allison pulled her knees to her chest and hugged them tightly. The chain linking her wrists together clanked loudly. She eyed the metal door directly in front of her.

*How long before they come back? What will they do?*

She imagined her body twig-thin from months of starvation, the bones of her elbows and knees grotesquely pronounced. Or maybe they'd beat her until her face was no longer recognizable as human. Or they might sit her at a table and ask pointed, twisted questions until she went crazy with their relentless voices in her head.

Allison rested her cheek on one knee. Fear crept into her heart and injected its disease into her blood so that her body trembled. Despair clouded her mind as she gazed at the harsh gray walls. She closed her eyes and searched desperately for hope inside herself. There was none.

Allison.

She looked at the door. It was inexorably closed.

*I'm going crazy.*

No, I am here.

Her body shook uncontrollably as fear escalated into panic. "Who's there?"

You called me, and I have come.

Bewildered, she searched for one moment of reality that might hush this voice in her head. A memory surfaced; a faceless man in black ground her prone body into the pavement while he rapidly captured her wrists in handcuffs. She had cried out...

Allison raised her head and whispered, "Jesus....?"

I am. Don't be afraid, little one.

"What do you want?"

I want your heart. And I want to give you mine. I want to be your savior, your comforter, your healer, and your father.

She shook her head slowly. "Why?" she breathed.

Deep laughter rolled pleasantly like a great wind in the trees.

Because I love you.

Allison was silent.

You don't believe me.

"No," she admitted, her back stiff against the wall. "I don't see any evidence of your love. Not here, not anytime in my life. If you loved me, you would've taken care of me."

I have always taken care of you.

Images from her past sifted through her mind; her four-year-old self squeezing in between two file cabinets at the BIO nursery, a hiding place no one ever discovered; a much larger boy about to hit her with a stick distracted by a fight exploding across the yard; the orphanage guards who did nothing more hurtful than yell at her; her successful escape from the orphanage and unhindered flight through the heart of the city; the horrible night of the failed rescue mission and the narrow escape from the GSD squad.

I have always been with you.

Into Allison's mind floated the round, beaming face of the one matron at the BIO nursery who always had a soft word and a hug for her, Yanna's pixie face, Faye, Zip, the Krueger family, and Papa.

Allison swallowed a sob, overwhelmed with the memories of

love.

"But why…. Why, if you love us so much, did you let them die? My friends, the other inferiors? ….My parents?"

He was silent. And then his sorrow fell like rain on her heart, heaved like waves through her entire being. She hunched over and cried with him.

*Oh, Allison, did you think I just let them die? Oh, my child, I love each and every one; I long for each and every one to be my child and to love me. Even those who have abused and tormented you. But I will not force them to do as I wish. I want a relationship – that is what I created people for, that we might enjoy one another. That is what I lived, died, and rose again for. It must be their choice, though it brings pain and tears.*

*But I will not wait forever. The time will come when I return to bring my enemies to justice and gather my children to come home with me. Until that day I am patient, always working events to my own good purpose.*

Allison's tears subsided at his tender words until she was only hiccupping lightly. She rubbed her nose and sniffed.

"Can I ask about now? Why I'm in this cell now?"

*We needed a place to talk, you and I.*

She stared incredulously at the wall before her.

*And I don't mean the location. Your heart did not hear me until I brought you through all those troubled times to this crucial point.*

Allison blinked at this unexpected answer. Embarrassed by her flippant words, and a little afraid that she'd offended him, she shifted on her seat and was silent.

*I love you.*

"I'm sorry," she whispered.

Tranquility descended lightly on her heart.

*And I forgive you. Will you let me in?*

"Yes."

A heady warmth spread through Allison's veins. It weighted her limbs so that she had to lie down, but it wasn't on chilly concrete; the warmth wrapped her skin and mind in its comfort.

Allison smiled and relaxed as his voice came again, whispering peace and healing and truth.

# 22

Dark, rich wood paneled the walls of the Director's office, accentuated by strategically placed can lights. The clean, sharp lines of black furniture stood out like artwork in the vast space. An oversized desk dominated the far wall, backed up by a throne-like chair. Allison's feet sank into the lush, gray carpet as two GSD agents escorted her to the center of the room. They each held one of her arms, and her hands dangled in front of her with the chains clinking in between. They stopped with an unnecessary jerk in the center of the room.

"We wait here," one of the men said.

Allison ignored him and continued to look around. The dimensions of this office were clearly meant to put little people in their places, but she was not afraid. Something else about it nagged at her mind. *It's very quiet. There are no smells. No, that's not it....*She hunched her shoulders as if something nasty had landed on them. *Evil.*

A panel in the back wall slid open noiselessly. From its black mouth emerged a trim man in a well-cut charcoal suit. Allison's guards tightened their iron grips and straightened their posture.

He glided forward, passing over his throne to lean casually against his desk. Allison was surprised by his apparent agelessness. She could see only a few fine lines around his eyes and mouth and a little silver streak in his immaculate hair. His eyes.... *Hard, flat stones in a cold face.* Allison shivered when she realized how intently those eyes were studying her.

"You look too young to make so much trouble," the Director observed. His quiet, diplomatic tones were shocking after the silence.

"I grew up fast," Allison rasped.

"Yes, the system worked well. We encouraged your intelligence in certain areas, and you were useful for a time." He crossed his arms and peered at her unpleasantly. "And then you escaped. How aggravating. I do hate loose ends, but now that we have you back we can tie them up very neatly."

"What do you want?"

The Director dropped his arms and came forward a few steps. "You were with the resistance long enough to learn a few things. Who is Papa?"

She blinked. "Papa?"

"Do you know the identity of Papa?" he asked again, unable to hide the eager edge in his voice.

Tell him the truth.

Puzzled, she turned her head a little to the side. *What...?*

Tell him the truth.

*Okay.*

"No," she said aloud. "I don't know who he is."

The Director examined her face for a long minute. She met his eyes steadily. He relaxed a little, smiling coolly.

"Pity. Well, it's only a matter of time. The resistance ring is broken, you know, thanks to the unfaltering diligence of one Robert Stokes. All your friends, including the family that sheltered you, have been taken into custody."

Lies.

Allison shifted. She stared directly into his enigmatic eyes and caught an odd gleam there.

"I don't believe you."

His composure cracked for an instant, his eyes snapping angrily at her before he regained control. "The orphanage years have made you tough as leather."

"What do you want?" she repeated.

"Oh, I just wanted to meet you before you die."

Allison met his gaze without so much as a wince. It was what she had expected, and she wasn't about to give him the reaction he wanted. The Director seemed amused by her lack of response and settled back against the desk. A triumphant glint in his eyes set off warning bells in her brain.

"It's a pity you weren't born Aryan," he said slowly. "A person like you could be a great success in this world."

"I don't want any part of your world. I've experienced all the cruelty you Germans have toward innocent people. I would be ashamed to be Aryan."

"Lovely sentiments. Let's speak to each other as equals, shall we? I don't subscribe to the lies about the Jews or anyone else. They're all quite human, and you in particular are one of the most intelligent I've come across. I admire that. I never underestimate human intelligence in any shape because I know the truth."

Allison's eyes narrowed. "What do you mean?"

"You think everyone has been brainwashed to believe you're an animal?" He shook his head and clicked his tongue. "Adolf Hitler was the author of that particular lie. He knew the potential of the uniting power of the scapegoat. It was necessary to unite people of such different customs as the Germanic peoples. Your ancestors were chosen to take the blame. It might have been anyone, but you got the raw end of the deal." He shrugged. "So sorry."

Allison blanched as the venom-coated truth seeped into her mind. It was all an elaborate charade. No common citizen would ever have lifted a finger to help, even if they knew the truth. Not because they were ignorant, but because they didn't care.

"I'm the ignorant one," Allison whispered. "You can kill millions of people because your hearts are rock-hard. But now there will be no one to trample, no one to force into slavery. No one to blame."

The Director rocked back and forth on his feet and regarded some distant point in time with satisfaction. "We're not finished with the world. We have yet to conquer a few continents. It will be a challenge to enjoy. My agents have grown bored with our peaceful situation. You and your friend gave us an intriguing little puzzle, which I thank you for."

"I can die knowing that I was of some use. Is that it?"

"Something like that, yes."

"But you'd rather I die with a broken heart and spirit. You prefer torture of the mind."

The Director nodded. "Perceptive. That is my preferred method. Good-bye, Allison. I enjoyed our conversation. Tell your parents how smart you were."

Allison winced under the impact of the blow.

"So sorry about the bad information in your file."

"You knew Zip would hack the system."

"I knew he couldn't resist."

"But you didn't know how good he is. We read about the adults, too." Tears blurred her vision in spite of her resolve to stay in control.

"Don't take it so hard. At least you weren't laboring under a false hope for long. And now you may return to your cell. It was very nice to meet you. Good-bye."

He smiled genially at her pain and defeat. He had taken her apart easily, as a malicious child would destroy an insect. The guards began to move backward. The Director turned slightly to pick up a memo, his prey dismissed from his mind.

*You are my child, and you have overcome him. Greater is he who is in you than he who is in the world.*

Allison's heart lightened and expanded with those whispered words. An involuntary smile tugged at the corners of her mouth. She stood firm against the guards' tugging.

"Director," she said clearly.

He looked up again, boredom covering his features.

"I just realized," she grinned, "you can't hurt me. You've lost. Your plan has failed."

The Director's face went blank.

The lightness within Allison bubbled up and surged out her

mouth. She laughed loudly, freely. The Director flushed scarlet, and the memo crackled as his hands began to shake. "Stop that!" he whispered fiercely.

"I feel sorry for you," she chuckled. "You have killed countless people for power, but you couldn't kill their souls. My soul doesn't belong to you. You can't even touch it."

His entire body shook with rage. "Stop laughing!" he spat. "Out! Get her out! Kill her *now*!"

Allison yielded to the guards' frantic pulls and left the Director to rant and shake by himself. One guard paused to close the door behind them, and the secretary outside stared at her through his metal-rimmed glasses. She smiled benignly at him and went quietly with her guards down the wood-paneled hall to the elevator. Down they rode, from floor 20 to the basement where the metal doors opened automatically.

There was only one cinder block hall illumined by weak yellow bulbs, and it led them to a flight of poured concrete stairs. Down that everlasting flight of stairs they went. Allison nearly smiled at the irony of it all. The GSD really did bury their skeletons – deep underground, as though they were ashamed of their activities. Burying the dead was perfectly normal in the civilian sphere. Trust the GSD to follow that tradition in their slinky, suspicious way.

Allison lost track of time and distance in that bleary, gray world. She stepped mechanically, the thump of her feet keeping time with the pulse of blood in her ears. They stopped at a door on a landing, and Allison quickly read the word "Lab" before it swung open.

They stepped into a long, white room illuminated by glaring lights. Allison blinked with temporary blindness and trusted the guards to guide her steps. They seemed eager to be rid of her, so she had little more than an impression of her surroundings. A wall of large metal lockers, deserted hospital beds clustered here and there.

*No*, she corrected herself, *they're just padded trays waiting to cart the next dead body away.* She looked quickly away.

Her escorts came to a halt by an alcove fitted out like the

nurse's lab at the orphanage. Metallic glitters caught at her vision from the white counters. A middle-aged man in a long, snowy jacket bent over an operating table, his forehead wrinkled in concentration.

"Doc, we got another one. Director says to take care of her now."

Allison went numb inside.

It was Zip's unruly hair poking out in every direction, Zip's impish face as pale as the sheet that enfolded him. Ugly blue bruises blotched his skin. One eye was grotesquely swollen, and a tear of blood dripped from a long cut that peeled back the skin of his left cheek.

He was dead.

A ragged sob broke from her chest. *God, NO!*

Trust me.

The balding doctor drew the sheet over Zip and straightened to greet his next victim. Sad, brown eyes regarded her through the shine of glasses. A white mask covered his mouth. He gestured toward the empty table on his other side, admonishing the uneasy men to be careful. Allison shuddered as they picked up her arms and legs and laid her on the cold steel. The doctor waved them off as he moved in to secure her to the table with thick black straps.

She sucked in the sterile air. *Please, are you still there?*

I am here. Be still, love.

Peace enveloped her as she watched the doctor stir a yellowish liquid in a slim glass tube. Gently he laid aside the stirring stick and transferred the concoction to a syringe. Deep lines creased his forehead and branched out from the corners of his eyes. Lines of sorrow.

"Why are you so sad?" she whispered.

His fingers paused.

"It's okay," she said gently.

The doctor padded to her side and gently rolled back her sleeve.

"This will sting at first," he said soothingly. "The nightmare will be over in a minute. Don't be afraid."

As the needle invaded her skin, Allison looked into those sorrowful eyes. Only now they were wide and intense, and he was whispering something through his mask. Her sluggish brain tried to form a question, but couldn't force it out. She listened, fascinated, to the lagging beat of her heart until it drowned it a deep black sea.

# 23

*T*his *can't be Heaven. It's too cold.*

Allison vaguely felt someone shaking her arm. Awareness grew of her shivering skin, chafing underneath a wool blanket. The tremors eased, and she took a deep breath.

*Breathing…. I'm supposed to be dead. What happened?*

You were never close to death.

*What? Why not? The doctor….*

I always leave a remnant.

Allison moved her head a little, unsure how to take his statement.

*A remnant. You could've mentioned that earlier.*

Yes, but you would not have played a very convincing death scene.

Allison smiled mentally. *Huh.*

She cracked open one eye, squeezed it shut as daylight lanced her vision. She gave herself a minute and tried again, squinting at two blurry faces hovering over her.

"She's coming around. Keep her warm, and don't let her talk a lot. Give her food when she wants it. Where's the water?"

The voice rolled over her in waves, familiar in its quiet assurance. Slowly the face of the doctor pieced itself together, this time with a sensitive mouth in place of the mask. He smiled in relief and patted her hand.

"Good-bye." He rose and walked into the blur of green and

brown and white.

Bristling hair and laughing green eyes intruded in her vision. She winced at the grotesque bruises and the bandages on Zip's face.

"Welcome back to the land of the living," he said. With a flourish he produced a metal thermos and gently poured cool water into Allison's parched mouth. She swallowed eagerly and savored the cold tingle that eased her throat.

"What happened?" she rasped as she tested her thick tongue against the roof of her mouth.

"You tricked death. Or rather, our sympathetic doctor did. He's been working with our resistance group for years. That injection he gave us causes our bodies to hibernate for a few days. It took a while to perfect it, but he's been sneaking people out of the GSD's lair ever since."

"Could've warned me."

"The lab is bugged, like all GSD offices. He couldn't say anything without ruining the whole operation. No more questions now. You're supposed to be quiet."

Allison glanced around and winced at the merry-go-round of pain that movement caused. Their doctor friend had brought them to a cemetery. Acres of old headstones poked from the ground at crazy angles, regarding the world with bone-white faces. The newer part was lumpy with unmarked graves. Stillness hovered over the cemetery in respect for the dead.

Zip helped her to stand in stages, poking fun at her moans and lack of balance.

"I bet you felt like this, too," she said as he settled a fleecy blanket over her shoulders.

"Yep. But I'm quick on the recovery. Now hush up."

Swaying unsteadily, they picked their way across the grass to a rusty blue pick-up slouching on the edge of the road. He helped her climb into the truck and tucked her in a small nest of blankets with the thermos of water in her lap. She curled up with a yawn, nodding off as the dilapidated truck popped and groaned to life.

She slipped in and out of consciousness the next few hours, dimly aware of bumps and squeaks. Once she woke briefly to Zip slapping the dashboard to silence an annoying rattle. In spite of its noisy protests, the truck held together.

At sunset Zip turned into a deeply rutted road and parked in a ditch. He jumped from the tilted vehicle and ran around it to extract Allison from her cocoon. She sat carefully in the cool grass and rolled up two blankets while he retrieved several small packs from under the seat. One fleecy blanket she swung around her shoulders against the chill that lingered around her bones.

"Shouldn't we hide the truck?" she asked dubiously.

"No. Someone will come get it tomorrow morning."

"Then this is a planned stop."

"Yep. We're gonna walk for a while. How're you feeling? Think you can do it?"

"I'm a little shaky. But I think I can walk."

They started at a slow pace, following the dirt road until it was too dark to see the potholes underneath the canopy of trees. Zip mumbled directions to himself and let Allison rest a minute while he got his bearings.

"What happened to you?" she asked, gesturing to his face.

"Ah." Zip tapped the long bandage that bisected his cheekbone. "The goons questioned me."

"Questioned! What did they want to know?"

"They wanted Papa -- his name and location, specifically. Or someone who could lead them to him."

"What did you say?"

"Nothing."

"So they hit you some more?"

"No, I ridiculed them, so they hit me some more. They quit before I died and dumped me back in my cell. Our friend the doctor heard about it. He forged some papers with the Director's signature releasing me for 'immediate termination.' And here I am."

Allison drew a breath. "That's weird."

"What's weird, miss, is how you totally escaped a beating.

What happened to you?"

Allison looked thoughtfully at the leafy branches overhead. "I guess I made the Director angry."

Zip eyebrows shot up. "Angry! *You* got under that man's skin? Allison, I played his cat and mouse game with him and lost. He pushed all my buttons with the ease of a professional typist and dismissed me to the cretin club for a beating. How did *you* get him angry?"

"I had help," she said simply. She related her experience with God in the cell and the details of her interview with the Director, punctuated with insights from that quiet voice. Disbelief was stamped all over Zip's face by the time she finished.

"You laughed at the Director? That's the most foolish thing I've ever heard. The only logical explanation is that you went slightly crazy in your cell and started talking to your own mind."

"No." Allison snuggled in her blanket and calmly met his demanding stare.

"Well, let's keep going," he said at last. "We should be there in a minute, and then you can rest all night."

Then they struck off across a bordering field, long weeds swishing about their legs. Just as the last remnants of color had faded from the sky, they emerged from the tall grass. A meadow of soft, perfect grass stretched out in the dusky half-light, its borders hedged by a barely discernible line of trees. A hushed chorus of crickets filled the air with their strange music. She closed her eyes for a second and found herself on the Kruegers' patio on a gently windy night.

"This is where we sleep," Zip gestured expansively, obviously pleased. "It's a genetic engineering experiment. A group of scientists created a hybrid of lawn grasses and planted the seeds out here. They only check on it every few months, so it's all ours."

Allison shook her head in wonder. She unfurled the blankets, wrapped herself in another one, and hunched down against the feathery blades. Zip stretched out on his back and began to nibble something crunchy. Allison felt a bit queasy at the thought of food and wordlessly refused the edible bar he offered. She turned back to the incredible scene before her.

It was so spacious, so peaceful it almost frightened her. Here the laws and lives of men seemed insignificant and futile. Gnarled trees counted the ages in lifetimes. Their branches twined ever upward, oblivious to the petty humans buzzing around them. Weeds grew unchecked in their silent war against neighbor plants, too resilient to be stamped out of existence. The stubborn weeds that grew through the cracked pavement of the old city came to Allison's mind. Man could manipulate, twist, and bend his surroundings, but his rules could never govern them.

Allison tilted her head back and gazed up at the vast night sky. Darkness trailed across it like a filmy cloud shading the mysteries of space. Pinpoints of light glowed dimly from their lofty positions, and the moon turned a tranquil face on the dreaming earth. Shivering under such majestic beauty, she remembered a few words from her little dog-eared Bible.

"'He wraps himself in light as with a garment; he stretches out the heavens like a tent and lays the beams of his upper chambers on their waters. He makes the clouds his chariot and rides on the wings of the wind....'"

"What are you muttering?" Zip's voice jarred her from her reverie.

"Something from the Bible. Ever read it?"

"Huh," Zip snorted.

*Don't worry, little one. I can open even a mind as tightly shut as his.*

Allison smiled mentally at his timing and the gentle humor of his tone.

"He's real," she insisted aloud.

"Right. Well, believe what you like. It's a free country out here."

"Free. What are we gonna do now that we're free?"

"We're off to South America, then to Australia. That's a huge island that's got the Nazis stumped. Can't count how many times they've tried to take it and failed miserably. We'll be safe there."

"Safe and happy while the GSD murders our friends."

197

Rolling to an elbow, Zip frowned at her. "I feel the same way, but let's be practical, Allison. These people sacrificed their safety to get us out. We're not leaving to protect ourselves. They're expecting us to help the South Americans and Australians find weak points in the GSD's facade. What we know could change the fate of the world. Nothing's more important than that."

Allison rested her chin on her knees, not caring about the scratchy wool blanket. She breathed in the peace that cloaked their little field and remembered the mission Papa had entrusted to her.

"I don't think that's the most important knowledge we have," she murmured.

Zip leaned forward again and rubbed her shoulder. "Hey, I'm sorry if I was harsh a minute ago. I won't preach at you again." He paused. "Forgive me?"

Allison couldn't keep from smiling. "Sure."

"You can't help it. I'm irresistible."

Allison's hand snaked out and knocked him over. Zip rolled into his blanket with a chuckle.

"Well, I'm tired." He yawned widely. "Good night, Allison."

"Good night, Zip."

"We're off to a free world tomorrow."

"Hmmm."

Allison curled up on her side and watched the grass nod in a slight breeze. The leaves whispered as her mind drowsed. *A free world. One where you ride a chariot made of clouds and wear the sun like a coat....* A cool wind brushed her cheek like a finger, and she shivered delightedly at the touch.

"My sheep listen to my voice; I know them, and they follow me.

I give them eternal life, and they shall never perish;

no one can snatch them out of my hand."

John 10:27-28

# About the Author

Marta Coffer grew up with an innate love of reading that quickly developed into a love for writing. She studied Imaginative Writing at Eastern Michigan University and now teaches high school writing classes at her local home school cooperative. She lives in Michigan with her husband and their children.

To learn more about Marta and her writing, visit her web site at: www.martacoffer.com.